Dominic looked hard and directly into her eyes. 'You see how out of touch we are with each other, Alexandra? There's nothing here for you any more.'

'So you say. But I have a right to know why I'm being shunned like a leper. You may believe it or not, as you choose, but I truly don't have any idea.'

'Then I should not be the one to tell you,' he insisted firmly. 'So far as I am concerned, the subject is closed. It would be better for you to forget it. I'm perfectly willing to lend you my apartment for a few more days, so long as I can foresee an end to the arrangement.'

Alexandra found that she was quivering with a rage she could hardly conceal. She would choke, she was convinced, if she had to sit at the table with this hateful, arrogant man, and eat.

'You may have your apartment back whenever you wish,' she declared coldly. 'Just let *me* know when you'd like to move back in, and I'll be out like a flash. You may be Comte d'Albigny, but you don't rule Perpignan these days, and you can't have me ridden out of town! You can't force me to leave!'

Another book you will enjoy by LEE STAFFORD

A PERFECT MARRIAGE

Marissa was devastated when she learned that Grafton Court, her ancestral home, was to be sold to an American who might well turn it into a commercial leisure park. There *was* a way out—but could she possibly marry the American, Rick Jablonski, just to keep her house a home?

A DREAM
TOO SWEET

BY

LEE STAFFORD

MILLS & BOON LIMITED
ETON HOUSE   18–24 PARADISE ROAD
RICHMOND   SURREY   TW9 1SR

All the characters in this book have no existence outside the imagination of the Author, and have no relation whatsoever to anyone bearing the same name or names. They are not even distantly inspired by any individual known or unknown to the Author, and all the incidents are pure invention.

All Rights Reserved. The text of this publication or any part thereof may not be reproduced or transmitted in any form or by any means, electronic or mechanical, including photocopying, recording, storage in an information retrieval system, or otherwise, without the written permission of the publisher.

This book is sold subject to the condition that it shall not, by way of trade or otherwise, be lent, resold, hired out or otherwise circulated without the prior consent of the publisher in any form of binding or cover other than that in which it is published and without a similar condition including this condition being imposed on the subsequent purchaser.

First published in Great Britain 1990 by Mills & Boon Limited

© Lee Stafford 1990

*Australian copyright 1990
Philippine copyright 1990
This edition 1990*

ISBN 0 263 76774 4

*Set in 10 on 12 pt Linotron Times
01-9008-50062
Typeset in Great Britain by Centracet, Cambridge
Made and printed in Great Britain*

CHAPTER ONE

ONLY as she switched off the engine of her hired car at the foot of the steps leading to Château Albigny was Alexandra aware of the first stirrings of apprehension. The last time she saw this place she had been a skinny schoolgirl of fifteen. Could she come back, unannounced, unexpected, as a woman of twenty-six?

That morning, in her hotel room in Perpignan, she had awoken thinking of Tristan, and the horror had come rushing back at her. Memories of those last fraught weeks, the urgent trip to the hospital, the desperate hours pacing the antiseptic corridors, and then the funeral...her mind had blanked out, refusing to take that hurdle.

Irrationally she had told herself, It will all be all right once I get to the château. The d'Albignys were her relatives, however distant; they would remember and welcome her, of course they would, in spite of the years of absence when there had been no communication between them.

Now, she was not so sure. Driving through the estate, with acre upon acre of vines either side of her, past the winery where the presses turned the heavy yield of grenache and syrah into the wines which bore the château's distinctive cream and gold label, it had all been instantly familiar, like coming home. And there was the house, its terracotta stone glowing warmly, sitting on a slight incline reached by a flight of stepped, terraced gardens. Behind it, the shady green of the plane trees, and the mountains beyond, the foothills climbing towards the high, distant peaks of the Pyrenees.

The sun was hot, the sky deep azure, and the house and gardens were wrapped in the deep hush of afternoon. Alexandra got out of the car and climbed the steps, her heart suddenly beating with jumpy irregularity. Here she had played with her French cousins as a child, summer after glorious summer. Here, when she was fifteen, she had fallen madly and uselessly in love with the eldest of them, her handsome cousin Dominic. Alexandra swallowed hard. He would have turned thirty now, and was probably a married man. He would have forgotten all about her moonstruck adoration. Adolescent love was painful, but the adult version hurt more, as she had every reason to know.

Alexandra rang the bell, hearing its sound disturb the silence within. She wouldn't ask for Dominic or his father, the Comte. She would ask to see the woman she had always known as Tante Corinne, Dominic's grandmother. A sprightly, energetic matriarch, she had always been the ruling force of the household, a proud, strong lady who had loved all the children, sorted out their problems, refereed their arguments, and always been ready to talk and to listen.

A maid in a black dress opened the door. '*Mademoiselle?*' she enquired politely, her raised eyebrows expressing surprise that a stranger should call, uninvited.

Alexandra cleared her throat, and in her best French asked, '*Est-ce-que Madame la Comtesse est à la maison?*'

'Madame la Comtesse is resting, *mademoiselle*,' the maid replied. 'She is not expecting any visitors today. Perhaps if you could leave your name...'

The girl was only doing her job, no doubt, but Alexandra could not face the prospect of being turned away now. Why, this house had once been a second home to her! She stepped smartly into the imposing black and white marble-floored hall, just as the maid was about to close the door on her.

'I've come all the way from England,' she said. 'I would be happy to wait until the Comtesse is ready to see me. If you could just tell her that Alexandra is here—Alexandra Warner.'

'But, *mademoiselle*——' The girl was obviously not used to callers who would not be told. The sound of their voices echoed in the high-ceilinged hall, and, at the far end, the double doors of the *salon* opened. There was a creaking sound as a wheelchair emerged, and Alexandra could not stifle a gasp of horrified amazement.

Tante Corinne, who had always been so spry and vigorous, in a wheelchair? It was she, sure enough. Older, her face more deeply lined, all streaks of black now vanished from hair which was iron-grey, thin-veined hands propelling the chair towards her.

'Oh, *madame*, I am so sorry to have woken you,' said the maid, distressed. 'But the young lady refused to leave, and...'

'Please—it's my fault, not hers,' Alexandra said quickly, addressing herself to the woman in the chair. 'I should have let you know I was coming, instead of simply descending on you.' She paused; the French she had not used for years was only hesitantly coming back to her. 'Perhaps you don't remember me? I'm Alexandra—Christine's daughter.'

Corinne d'Albigny had obviously been dozing in her chair, and her eyes as she stared at Alexandra were at first unfocused and puzzled. Then they cleared, and hardened, and there was no mistaking the icy disdain in their depths.

'I can see very well who you are,' she said, coldly and clearly. 'The resemblance is too strong to miss! How dare you show yourself here?'

Alexandra felt as if she had been slapped hard across the face for no apparent reason. She had expected a welcome, but Tante Corinne was treating her like an enemy, not a long-lost relative.

'I don't understand,' she began helplessly. 'There must be some mistake. Please—can we talk?'

The old lady's hands began to shake violently, and she gripped the arms of her chair tightly. 'Get out of my home! Get out—and don't come back!' she snapped.

Alexandra could not move. She was afraid that, if she tried to take a step, she would collapse. The thin veneer of her own composure was already threatening to crack under the strain recent months had put on it, and now this was the last straw.

Tante Corinne must have mistaken her immobility for defiance. 'Dominic!' she cried, raising her voice in a desperate appeal. 'Dominic—help me!'

'*Attendez, Grand-mère! Je viens tout de suite!*'

Dominic? The man's voice, deep but melodious, came from somewhere at the top of the flight of stairs which led up from the hall, and, instinctively, Alexandra's gaze locked, fascinated, as its owner descended them with swift, agile grace.

He'd been tall as a boy, but thinner; now, although he still possessed the slim matador's hips, his shoulders had broadened. How well she remembered his thick, dark hair, the kind that needed to be well and frequently cut. Even then, he could look remote and austere until he smiled; she had never known a face on which the smile—brilliant, dazzling, often mischievous—could make such a difference, but he was not smiling now, and manhood had created hard lines around his mouth and across his brow. His eyes were the most memorable feature, still. They were raven-dark, the irises almost luminous—the d'Albignys had the blood of Saracen princelings in their ancestry, it was said. Those eyes were sharp and perceptive now, raking her suspiciously.

Her adolescent romantic attachment to him was so far back in the past that she had thought it would have ceased to have any relevance. Why, then, did she feel as if someone had thumped her hard and taken away her breath? Why could she neither tear her gaze away from him, nor find her voice to speak?

Her mother and his father had been cousins, and she had always called him cousin Dominic. He had taught her to swim and to ride, beaten her at chess and tennis, and he had been—reluctantly, it must be said—her first love. With an effort, Alexandra forced her mind back to her present predicament. Surely he could sort this out? She held out a hand to him in frantic appeal.

'Dominic! You remember me, don't you? Thank goodness you're here! I don't understand what's happening. What's wrong?'

Her plea went unanswered. 'Young lady,' he said grimly, his voice hard and uncompromising, 'you are upsetting my grandmother, and I must ask you to leave. Let's have you on your way.'

He took her arm in a painful, unceremonious grip, and virtually frogmarched her down the hall. Her leaden feet had no option but to move to his directive as he swiftly and purposefully marshalled her out of the house, and, at an authoritative nod from him, the maid closed the door behind them.

'Now, then,' he said curtly, addressing her in English as precise and fluent as her own, 'I don't know what you hoped to gain by turning up here, out of the blue. If your intention was not malicious, the best explanation I can give is that you're damned insensitive!'

She tried, but failed, to shake loose the hand that still gripped her arm. 'Gain? Malicious?' she repeated blankly. 'I haven't the faintest idea what you're talking about!'

'Either you're very naïve, or I'm the President of France!' he said sceptically. 'Do you really expect me to believe that?'

Alexandra could not take it in. Her beloved Tante Corinne, who had once treated her as if she were another of her grandchildren, had looked on her with loathing and ordered her out of the house. And Dominic, who had been her favourite cousin, with whom she had shared a special and treasured friendship until that last summer, when her budding womanhood had made her all too painfully aware of him—Dominic was lambasting her with cold sarcasm, and hurting her—*hurting her!*

It could not be true—she must have strayed into some weird nightmare!

'Let me go!' she demanded, emotion thickening her voice.

'I'll let you go—indeed, I shall insist that you go—when I'm sure you're going to get back in your car and take yourself right back where you came from,' he said. 'My grandmother is not in good health, she's old, and has enough to contend with. I won't have her worried or made unhappy. I suggest you leave, now, without making a fuss, and don't attempt to come back here, or to get in touch with her. Is that clear?'

Clear? It was totally incomprehensible! The only thing about which there could be no mistake was that she was quite definitely not wanted.

The world began to dissolve around her, the colours of the sky, the trees, the mountains running into one, like water-colours too thinly applied, and she swayed a little, feeling the panicky sensation of ebbing self-control. She wrenched her arm from his grasp. Somehow, it was important that he did not suspect this fraility in her. This time he allowed her to break free, and she turned and ran, stumbling, down the steps to her car. Opening the door, she all but fell into the driver's seat, but it was no use—she could do no more. Alexandra collapsed over the steering-wheel, her thick, unruly fall of russet-gold hair drooping forward to conceal her face, her slim shoulders heaving.

The car door opened. Even through the mists of her distress, she was acutely aware of his presence.

'Move over,' commanded Dominic d'Albigny.

'Go away. Just leave me alone,' she muttered, without raising her head. She remembered him as a lively, exuberant young man. How had he metamorphosed into this brusque, unsympathetic individual?

How he managed it she never knew, but, somehow, he manoeuvred himself inside the car, his hands sliding easily beneath her and lifting her bodily. One hand curved beneath her knees, the other supported her back, fingers spread over her ribcage, with the thumb resting lightly just below her breast. They were so close in the confined interior of the car that it felt dangerously like an embrace, and Alexandra was shocked by her own instant and unexpected response.

She jerked her head up, as if she would have struggled free, then stopped; something other than the strength of his arms held her transfixed, and her startled grey-green eyes gazed into the unrevealing darkness of his. So close. . .she saw the line of his mouth, less hard than she had thought, the curve of his lips hinting at compassion, humour, the full male sensuality which years of unknown experience had brought him. She saw the faint line of a scar on his left temple, legacy of a daredevil riding accident long ago, and recalled how profusely it had bled, how he had hated all the fuss it had caused. Her hand itched to touch that mark, to confirm this man as the boy she had loved. But he wasn't! And she had come to this moment with a woman's knowledge, not the innocence of a girl.

She remembered another moment, one she had perhaps never really forgotten, just pushed to the back of her mind, long ago, afraid to think about it. They had been stabling the horses after a ride, alone with the scent of hay and tack and each other's young bodies. He'd helped her down from her horse, and, as her feet touched the ground, she had daringly given way to an urge which had plagued and troubled her all summer, which she had been sure he must have been able to sense, but had carefully ignored whenever he was near her.

Instead of moving away, she had stayed in the circle of his arms, her body pressed against his, her hands resting on his shoulders. His sudden, sharply indrawn breath had filled her with a sweet relief and triumph—yes, he's in love with me, too, he *must* be! She had lifted her face to his, recklessly abandoned to whatever must follow, his head had bent towards hers, his lips very nearly brushing her mouth. . .she had ached with the nearness, not knowing what to do, but eager to learn. . .

And then it had been gone. He'd let her go, turned away, saying briskly, 'Be a good girl, Lexi, and rub the horses down.' Her eyes had flooded with tears, from the youthful humiliation of knowing that he hadn't really wanted her at all. She wasn't pretty enough, that must be it! There must be scores of girls at college with him who would be as willing as she, and who were prettier. Why should he bother with her?

She had rushed indoors, not wanting him to see that she had been going to cry, and had run up to her bedroom, where she had found her mother—packing, hastily stuffing Alexandra's clothes into her suitcase. She'd scarcely noticed her daughter's tearful face—her own had been set and closed, hardly less happy.

'Oh, good. There you are. Finish this—we're leaving,' Christine Warner had said briefly.

'Leaving? Now? But why. . .what. . .? We *can't*!'

'Hurry up, Alexandra. Don't argue. Just get a move on. I'll ring for a taxi.'

They had been out of the château within half an

hour. There had been no time to say goodbye to Dominic, or even to see him again.

So long ago, and it all flashed through her mind now, as if his touch had reawakened the memory. And here she was, in his arms again, the warm pressure of his thigh against her, the slight movement of his thumb on her breast stirring feelings she had thought were dead. She couldn't breathe or speak, afraid that the least motion, even a breath of air, would break the spell. . .

And then he broke it himself, depositing her firmly in the passenger seat as if she were not a woman but a sack of potatoes he was finding it tiresome to hold.

'It's fairly obvious you are in no state to drive,' he said coolly. 'Where to?'

'I'm staying in Perpignan. But I can manage to get myself there, thank you.'

He treated this declaration with cold scorn. 'Fasten your seatbelt.'

He turned the key in the ignition and set off down the private road amid the bright green sea of vines, away from the château, taking the corners swiftly and expertly. Clearly he could not get her off the estate quickly enough to suit him.

Indignation began to boil inside her. Who did the d'Albignys think they were, to turn her away so unkindly, without even a word of explanation? Huddled in the corner of her seat, shaken and humiliated, but still trembling with the aftermath of the sensations that their brief contact had induced in her, Alexandra fumbled in her handbag for her cigarettes and lighter.

He cast her a look of sheer distaste. '*Must* you do that?'

'It's not your car. You don't have to drive me,' she reminded him coldly. In response, he wound down the window, the incoming breeze effectively preventing the lighter flame from working. She glared at him. Was he always this unpleasant and dictatorial these days? Come to think of it, he always did have a fondness for getting his own way.

Briefly, her thoughts flew to Tristan, how much he had relied on her and needed her, and a fresh wave of self-pity shook her. No one needed or loved her now—there *was* no one. She glanced quickly at the man beside her. It was difficult to imagine *him* ever needing anybody; he seemed the epitome of independent arrogance.

He can't treat me like this, she thought furiously, and that boiling, seething sensation inside her reached a pitch where she had to say something or explode.

'Don't you think you owe me an explanation?' she demanded jumpily, shifting her position, crossing and recrossing her legs, her hands twisting nervously in her lap.

He laughed, but without any humour. 'I doubt I owe you anything,' he said. 'You came uninvited—why did you do that, unless, indeed, you were unsure of your welcome? Did you think you could just walk back in, after so long—in spite of everything?'

'In spite of what?' she cried, half turning towards him in her seat. 'All right, I should have phoned or written first. I don't know why I didn't.'

She bit her lip. How could she admit to someone already disposed to think the worst of her that she had left England in a state of mental near-exhaustion, knowing only that she had to get away, somewhere, anywhere...that she had bolted, and, when one bolted, one did not always prepare the ground? But that did not excuse the way she had been treated.

Suddenly a thought occurred to her. Tante Corinne was getting old, and sometimes strange things happened to people at that stage in their lives. It was sad to think that the proud old lady might be senile, her once sharp wits playing unfair tricks on her...but it was a possible explanation, the only one which made any sense. The only one which justified Dominic's reluctance to discuss it. Whatever his faults, she knew that he had always loved his grandmother dearly, and obviously still did.

She sighed. 'OK. You don't have to say any more.'

'I wasn't about to.'

Alexandra bit back a sharp retort. He could at least have met her halfway, could have shown some appreciation of her understanding. Was she to hope that, on a better day, Tante Corinne might want to see her? But Dominic had sounded so positive that this could not be. 'Don't attempt to come back...or get in touch,' he had said.

The few miles down the main road had flown by, and already he was easing the car swiftly into the busy flow of traffic crossing the bridge over the River Tet into Perpignan.

'Where's your hotel?' he asked shortly.

'The de la Gare. Near the station—obviously enough.'

Alexandra had arrived in the early hours of that morning, and exhaustion was beginning to tell on her. It was October, and this late in the year she had been unable to fly direct to Perpignan. She had flown to

Montpellier and had caught a train from there. But, even after the night porter had shown her to her room, she had been too keyed up to sleep. Anyhow, sleep had become something of a luxury to her during the time she had been at Tristan's beck and call when he was ill and disturbed; her body—and, even more so, her mind—had not been able, yet, to resume a regular pattern. She looked bleakly at the hotel's façade as Dominic pulled up outside. Another awful night loomed ahead of her, and still she was alone. More alone than ever now.

She got out of the car and so did he, handing her the keys.

'Thank you for the lift,' she forced herself to say politely. 'How will you get back to the château?'

'No problem. Don't worry about it.'

She should have gone straight inside, but automatically she opened the car boot and lifted her suitcase out. His eyes lit on it, and an expression of scornful amazement gleamed briefly in them.

'You brought your luggage along? Had you seriously expected to be asked to stay at the château?' he asked incredulously.

Alexandra banged the boot shut loudly, and fumbled to lock it with nervous fingers, clumsily dropping her suitcase on to the road as she did so. All her nerves were screaming, her responses were so jangled she could scarcely think straight any more, and, deny it as she might, for some reason he exacerbated the problem by his mere presence. But, tired and distraught as she was, something was nagging away at the back of her mind. She knew that there was something which did not add up.

He bent to pick up her case, and she snatched at it quickly before he could do so.

'Don't bother. I can manage,' she insisted jumpily.

'So you keep on saying. I don't see much evidence of it.'

She came close to hating him in that moment—his swift, perfect co-ordination of mind and body, his unassailable confidence in his own decisions and the rightness of all he said and did. How could anyone be *that* sure, *that* untroubled by doubts or weaknesses?

'Go to hell,' she said clearly. 'I don't know why I ever came back here. I must have been crazy.'

Turning her back on him, she stalked into the hotel without another word, and it took all of her remaining strength to explain to the girl on the reception desk that, although she had checked out that morning, her plans had changed and she wanted the room for another night, after all.

The receptionist was apologetic. 'I'm sorry, *mademoiselle*. The room has been re-let, I'm afraid.'

'Any room, then. It doesn't matter,' Alexandra said impatiently.

'But, *mademoiselle*, I'm afraid we don't have any. A special excursion has just come in, all booked in advance, you understand? Would you like me to telephone some other hotels for you?'

Alexandra's hand flew to her forehead. All she wanted now was to lie down, somewhere quiet, away from questions and decisions. How much more could she take?

'I. . . I don't know. . .' she murmured faintly.

'Come along.' A quiet, resigned voice spoke from behind her, and a hand took her suitcase from her.

Alexandra spun round and looked into the dark, unsmiling face of her cousin Dominic. 'I know somewhere you can stay.'

'I thought you had gone,' she said lamely.

He took her arm, and, in spite of her exhaustion and the muddled situation in which she had landed herself, she felt it once again: the shock, the thrill of contact.

'It was a good thing I hadn't,' he said, shepherding her firmly out of the hotel and back to the car.

Resentment flared up in her anew. He seemed to think she was a complete imbecile who could do nothing for herself. 'I'm not helpless, you know—just tired,' she said stiffly.

'*D'accord*.' The comment neither agreed nor contradicted. 'Give me the car keys.'

She hesitated briefly and he said, 'Don't be silly—I know Perpignan better than you do, particularly behind the wheel of a car.'

Alexandra found herself once more in the passenger seat, being driven by him along the plane- and cypress-fringed boulevards of the city. She glimpsed the cool waters of the canal which ran through the centre lined by wide avenues and shops, and, when he turned past a large, circular medieval building of warm red brick, memory stirred in her.

'That's the Castillet,' she said. 'We're in the old city.'

A maze of narrow streets barely wide enough for cars to pass spread out from here in all directions. Venerable old buildings housed intriguing shops of all kinds, cafés spilled out on to the pavements, full of people laughing and drinking in the warm sunshine. And then they were in a quieter area, more residential, less familiar to Alexandra, although Dominic seemed to know this fascinating warren like the back of his hand. She sat bolt upright, warning signals flashing red alert in her brain.

'Where are we going? I don't see any hotels around here.'

'Relax. I'm not going to sell you into slavery,' he said, amused, pulling up in a quiet square with a single large tree planted in its centre. High, four-storeyed buildings of ancient stone surrounded it, wooden shutters at all the windows; little streets led mysteriously off, to who knew where? There was a *boulangerie* on one corner, a tiny café with two iron tables outside on another.

He carried her case and she accompanied him apprehensively from the brightness outside into the cool, dark lobby of a building, where a concierge sat knitting in a minuscule office.

'*Bonjour*, Monsieur le Comte,' the concierge sang out cheerfully.

'*Bonjour, madame*,' Dominic replied, and, taking Alexandra's arm, propelled her into a lift barely large enough for the two of them. Obliged to stand very close to him, she could not help but note the smooth texture of his pale olive skin, with just a hint of shadow around the jaw, and the warm scent emanating from him, a combination of sharp, musky aftershave and masculinity.

They were almost as close now as they had been on that afternoon in the stables, and Alexandra wished furiously that she could stop thinking of that. It had nothing at all to do with her present life, her current problems. What did it matter if he had once rejected her young love? His entire family was turning its back on her cry for help now.

The lift cranked to a halt, debouching them on to the top floor, and she had to admit, in fairness, that her censure was not wholly true. He could, she supposed, have let her risk killing herself driving back to Perpignan in her distraught state. He could have left her to fend for herself at the Hôtel de la Gare. What had prevented him? *Noblesse oblige?* A lingering sense of family responsibility? Alexandra's lips twisted in a bitter little smile as she watched him turn his key in the lock and push open the door facing them.

From an inner vestibule they entered a spacious room furnished with vast leather sofas piled with varicoloured cushions, plants as big as young trees growing in shining brass tubs, tables topped with marble, mosaic or inlaid, damascened copper, lending more than a hint of the East. There was a huge stove imprisoned behind decorative glass doors, and the shutters were already half closed against the brilliant sun just beginning to fade into late afternoon.

Alexandra looked around her, and her gaze returned suspiciously to the man who had brought her here. She had taken it for granted that he lived at the château, but there were few men of his age who hadn't a place of their own, and this, obviously, was his. Equally obviously, he did not have a wife.

'I can't stay here with you,' she said bluntly.

A roguish grin gave the sombre features a piratical expression. 'Wait until you're asked,' he advised amusedly. 'There's no need to worry—you'll be alone here. I'm...not using it at the moment. I think you'll find there's everything you're likely to need. Bedroom and bathroom through here, kitchen that way.'

All the rooms led off the inner vestibule, and Alexandra followed him as he carried her case into the bedroom he had indicated. Doubt and uncertainty were written all over her face, a face perhaps too fine-boned and original for conventional beauty, but possessing a haunting, elusive quality. She looked like an abandoned waif.

'Look,' he said impatiently, 'you can please yourself. It's nothing to me, but you need a place to crash out, and this seems the easiest solution. What's the problem? Are you worried in case I've turned into a mass rapist since we last met?'

Alexandra's pale redhead's skin flushed uncomfortably. She was a grown woman who had lost the man she loved, not a frightened virgin, but, meeting those gently mocking eyes, she suddenly felt as much a débutante as she had that day in the stables. As if all the intervening years of living had never been.

'Of course not,' she said curtly. She had to stop thinking about that time. They were both other people now.

'Good,' he said. 'I'll just make some coffee, and then I'll leave you to it.'

Alexandra sat warily on the edge of the bed and gazed around her. A guest bedroom, plain and understated, in direct contrast to the living-room. Pine furniture, small-print Laura Ashley curtains and duvet cover. She tried hard to concentrate on her surroundings, to hide the fact that she felt ill at ease and uncomfortable, half resentful, half afraid of this aloof, scornful and only occasionally humorous man her cousin had become.

Rummaging in her handbag, she fished out a pack of cigarettes and the lighter which had been Tristan's. She struggled to produce a flame—the blasted thing was on the blink, as always—and had just got it going when Dominic entered, carrying a steaming cup of coffee.

The straight, elegant d'Albigny nose wrinkled with disapproval. 'That's a disgusting habit,' he remarked, disappearing into the living-room to return with an ashtray. 'However, I do have friends who smoke, although not normally in the bedroom.'

Until very recently, Alexandra had shared his aversion. She had picked up the habit from Tristan, who had been able to get through forty or more on a bad day, and she told herself that it calmed her nerves and that she would give it up just as soon as she felt better. Now a quiver of rebellion ran through her, and she puffed away definatly.

'You're the one who will have to sleep in this polluted atmosphere.' He shrugged, hooking both hands casually into the pockets of his impeccably cut trousers. 'Drink your coffee. It will do you, if not good, at least less harm.'

He left her alone then, and she heard him moving about quietly in the living-room. Endless questions raced through her mind. Why had he brought her here, and where was he going? What was it about him which succeeded in piercing the shell of misery in which she had existed for months, briefly stinging her back to awareness whenever she looked into his sceptical dark eyes, or felt the casual touch of his hand?

But, in spite of this tumult of thought and the build-up of nervous anxiety inside her, fatigue took its toll. Her head sank on to the pillow, her eyelids fluttered and closed. She didn't see him come in, stub out the cigarette she had left smouldering in the ashtray and remove the half-drunk cup of coffee. Already, Alexandra was fast asleep.

CHAPTER TWO

ALEXANDRA had left England on a raw, early October day when the wind was already whipping the leaves from the trees, and the chill of approaching winter could all too easily be felt.

'I do feel, my dear,' the dean of her Oxford college had said to her, quite kindly, 'that a break from all this would do you good. Without prying too closely into your private life, one is aware you have had a difficult time. You're reading for a PhD, after all, and you won't do it justice until your mind is clear. Get right away for a while.'

Alexandra had smiled bleakly. Both her parents were dead, she had no brothers or sisters, and her only friends were fellow students and colleagues right here, all of whom were occupied with their own work. She had wondered what he would suggest—a fortnight's package to Majorca?

'Have you no family you could go to—none at all?' he had asked.

'The only relatives I have are distant cousins who live in southern France, and whom I haven't seen for years,' she had said.

'However distant, there's nothing like family in a crisis,' the dean had said gently. 'And you would certainly have some sun,' he had added, with a wry glance out of the window at the lowering sky.

Alexandra had walked slowly through the courtyards

and quadrangles, thinking back to those long-ago childhood summers. Riding and swimming, fishing in the river, helping the workers in the vineyards—or, more often, getting under their feet. Huge lunchtime picnics under the trees, and grander feasts in the evenings, seated around the enormous table in the dining-room, everyone talking at once and eating with great appreciation. Her mother's glowing face—funny how she had always seemed to come to life in France, as if a lamp had been lit within her.

It was years since Alexandra had thought of Château Albigny. Her life had been taken up by studying, and then there had been Tristan. But now that the spark had been touched, she could not put it out of her mind. Why not? she had thought. On a mad impulse she had gone into a town centre travel agent's office and made her travelling arrangements.

It might have been distinctly autumnal back home, but here in this southernmost Mediterranean corner of France, close to the Spanish border, it was still summer, and in these lands where the sun was so bright, so early, shutters at the windows were a necessity. Alexandra, surfacing in Dominic's apartment after a sleep so profound she could not recall waking once, or even dreaming, was disorientated by the artificial darkness. Was it morning, or the middle of the night?

Struggling to a sitting position, she peered at the illuminated dial of the watch on her wrist. It was eight ten a.m. She had slept right through! Alexandra could not remember the last undisturbed night she had spent. Usually she was making tea, smoking and pacing the floor at four o'clock.

She got up, groped her way into the living-room

where the shutters were only half closed, and opened them fully to the brilliant day. Two of the windows were, in fact, doors opening out on to a huge, sheltered wrap-around balcony. From here, she looked out, not on to the square from which they had entered the building yesterday, but over the jumbled roof-tops to a distant panorama of tawny hills, beyond the far fringes of the city.

Of Dominic, of course, there was no sign. 'You'll be alone here. . . I'll leave you to it,' he had said. But where had he gone—back to the château? Glancing down at one of the small tables, a sheet of paper caught her attention, and she saw that he had left her a note.

> Cousin Alexandra,
> You may as well use my apartment for a few days. There is plenty of food and drink—feel free to help yourself to both. The concierge knows you are here, the *boulangerie* on the corner is rarely closed, and the café is a *bar-tabac* which sells newspapers as well. I've returned the car to the hire company. Enjoy Perpignan, but keep away from Château Albigny. I'll be in touch.
> Dominic.
> PS Don't smoke in bed.

Alexandra's cheeks burned at this mixture of solicitude and warning. As if she would dream of going back to the château, after her unfriendly reception yesterday! But since she could not go there, or even phone, he had left her no means of contacting him. How long was she supposed to stay here? 'A few days'? Until he showed up and turned her out? He had not offered to act as her host in any way. Family feeling obviously did not extend that far, she thought wryly. But he had left her a key—a heavy brass thing on a chain which probably weighed half a ton!

Alexandra went into the kitchen—small but modern, with a full complement of labour-saving devices fitted into its galley-like shape, and a shelf-ful of cookery books—and switched on the coffee percolator. She tapped her fingers thoughtfully on the marble work-surface as her mind went back over the events of yesterday, and, once again, that feeling of things not adding up correctly, of a puzzle with a piece missing, came back to her.

She saw that in her overemotional, exhausted state she had grasped at an explanation that sounded easy, but had to be wrong. Tante Corinne was not senile. She had been woken from a nap by Alexandra's arrival, and might have been briefly confused, but the old lady's wits, she was ready to swear, were as sharp as they had ever been. The ill-feeling, the enmity in her eyes and her voice, were not the products of a wandering mind.

She heard again Dominic's voice saying coldly, 'Did you think you could just walk back in after so long—in spite of everything?' as if she should have known she would be unwelcome, and knew than that, whatever was wrong, it had something to do with that last, long-ago visit.

She frowned. It surely could not be her innocent involvement with Dominic. No one had known about that but herself; she had not even confided in his sister Danielle, who had been her great friend in those days. It had been at one and the same time too important and too puzzling to talk to anyone about. Besides, nothing had actually happened to cause such a fuss. A silly teenage girl had fallen in love with a boy, and he had politely but coolly let her know that there was nothing doing!

No—it was something to do with her mother, she reasoned, remembering that desperate flight from the château. There must have been a quarrel, and she, too absorbed in her own disturbing adolescent trials, had been totally unaware of it. But one hell of a disagreement it must have been, to have left a residue of bitterness which had lingered for so many years—and rebounded on someone who had had no part in it!

Alexandra had struggled through her final year at school, trying not to dream about her cousin Dominic too much but hoping desperately that, next summer, things would be different. Perhaps he would find her prettier—was she prettier? She had squinted and frowned at herself in the mirror, not very hopefully.

But, when summer had come around, her mother had announced bluntly that they would not be going to France that year. 'I think we have outgrown it,' she had said. 'It was different when your father was alive, and we went as a family.'

'But we went last summer, after Daddy died,' Alexandra had protested. 'I don't think Daddy liked Château Albigny very much, anyhow; he never used to stay very long. We *must* go! Please! We *must*.'

'Alexandra. You are old enough to understand these things a little better now. The d'Albignys are a very aristocratic old family. We are only connected to them by virtue of your grandmother's marrying a British Special Operations Officer during the war. Even though your grandfather, Major Warner, was something of a war hero who had parachuted into occupied

France, that marriage was barely tolerated. They virtually had to elope,' Christine had said acidly. 'We're poor relations, so far as they are concerned; not really good enough.'

'We've been good enough up to now. I can't see what's changed,' Alexandra had argued heatedly. But it had made no difference. They had not gone back that summer, and they had never gone back again.

Something had died in Alexandra. . .or perhaps, having just begun to blossom in France, its growth had been stunted and cut off. The quiet, uncertain adolescent had become a studious, clever girl destined for educational heights, with neither time nor inclination for youthful romance.

Christine, too had never been the same again after that, Alexandra realised now, looking back. As mother and daughter they had not been especially close and confiding; they had seemed to drift even further apart. Her mother had withdrawn into herself, had been reserved and apathetic, as if the impetus of life had drained from her. During the winter of Alexandra's first undergraduate year at Oxford, Christine had caught pneumonia and had not recovered from it.

I never really knew her, Alexandra thought, watching the steam rise from her mug of coffee. She never allowed me to. What was it that happened that summer, to cut us off so completely? When he accepted the fact that she truly did not know, surely Dominic would tell her?

Thinking of Dominic was only slightly less puzzling than musing over the past—indeed, they were interconnected. She prowled restlessly around the apartment, trying to learn something of the man through his surroundings, and it seemed to her that there was a side to his personality which was...well, unusual, to say the least. Wasn't his taste in furnishings slightly bizarre?

There was a bathroom completely tiled in gleaming black, with a sunken, circular black bath and gold taps, which made her blink at its stark sensuality. But even that was as nothing compared to the master bedroom, which was decorated in a deep, intense shade of purple, with a gold-figured silk wall covering, velvet drapes, gold-fringed, heavy, purple satin sheets on the vast bed, and intricate, gold eastern-inspired lamps.

Alexander gasped out loud. What kind of a man slept in this flamboyant, eccentric potentate's hide-out? One wall was completely taken up by mirror-fronted wardrobes, and she could not resist sliding the doors. Inside there were expensively tailored suits, designer-label casuals, cashmere sweaters, pure silk shirts. Scarves, ties, Italian handmade leather shoes were neatly stacked on racks. She retreated hurriedly. Clothes were intensely personal. So were bedrooms, come to that, and she should not be in his.

Suddenly she felt the need to get out of here, quickly, before the personality of the man who owned all this threatened to swamp her.

She showered swiftly, put on a pair of clean Levis and a shirt and sandals, slipped the key into her pocket and closed the door of this strange new world resolutely behind her.

'*Bonjour, mademoiselle!*' the concierge sang out as Alexandra emerged from the lift. She wondered exactly what Dominic had told her about the woman occupying his apartment, but replied politely and hurried out.

In the streets around the Castillet she still vaguely knew her way, despite the many years that had passed since she last strolled through them. Past the Cathedral St Jean, through the Place Gambetta, uphill towards the Place de la République, memory guided her and she could still easily find her way back. But by now she had ceased to take note of where she was going. She simply kept on walking, omitting to observe street names or the number of times she turned left or right, lost in thought.

After Dominic, and that painful calf-love, there had really been no one for many years. The university had become her world, and it was there, last year, that she had met Tristan, who had come to lecture undergraduates at the same college where she had been studying for her master's degree.

As a young man he had had brief, meteoric success as a poet, but for some reason the spark had gone out and he had written nothing for years. The word about campus had been that his marriage had failed badly, and that he had a tendency to drink too much. But Alexandra had admired his earlier work very much, thought it a crying shame that such talent should have burned itself out without trace, and had been flattered when he had made a point of seeking her out.

'I've been watching you—you've been pointed out to me as an excellent student, and I know you have a first-class mind,' he had said. 'I wouldn't ask this of just anyone, but I wonder how you'd feel about doing a bit of research for me during the long vacation? It's for one of my courses. I'd do it myself, but...this is strictly between the two of us, but I feel the need to get on with some proper writing.'

Alexandra had felt a thrill run through her. Proper writing? That could only have meant that, after so many sterile years, he had been going to write poetry again, and he had wanted her to help him by lightening his burden. How could she have dreamt of refusing such an honour?

She had spent most of her vacation in the library, and in his flat, where he had lived alone in shambolic chaos. It had pained her to see him neglecting himself thus, and all her protective, womanly instincts had been aroused. She had spruced and tidied, she had cooked meals, she had researched. . .and, after the first, shocked occasion on which she had seen him drunk and abusive, she had rallied, told herself that it was not his fault, and that once the poetry started to flow he wouldn't need inspiration from a bottle. Meanwhile, she had hidden them, or poured away the contents, and had kept him from harm's way as well as she could.

'I need you, Alexandra—don't leave me,' he had begged her. 'That bitch I married and divorced emasculated me! I couldn't string two lines together after she'd done with me! You're so different. But how can I write poetry with all this lecture preparation to do. . .?'

By then Alexandra had begun to work for her PhD degree on Victorian women poets, but she had not seen how she could have abandoned Tristan. In her absence, he had gone to pieces. He had smoked too much, drunk heavily, and hadn't done any work. She had reached and passed the point where she could have denied him anything, and she had prayed that his students and the college authorities would never know how many of his lectures were prepared by her.

That she had been neglecting her own work, that his drinking had not only been ruining his health, but making *her* sick with worry on his behalf, that her own nerves had been strained to breaking-point by his sudden and alarming mood swings—well, dimly, she had known all this, but she had loved him, and love did not count costs.

Wrapped in the remembered anguish of lost love and heartbreak, Alexandra had lost all track of where she was, and, coming back suddenly to the present, she saw that she had wandered away from the well-trodden streets of fashionable boutiques and cafés which were well frequented by tourists into a part of the old city which was strange to her. The cobbled streets here were no wider than alleys. They were closed in by tall, secretive houses with lines of washing strung between high windows. The people who lived here were different, too—whip-slim, dark-eyed men who eyed her suspiciously, women in long Arab robes, their hands patterned with henna. She passed a dim, cavernous little Algerian restaurant and caught a whiff of exotic spices, then she was in a street market, like a *souk*, with stalls of strange vegetables and eels wriggling, still live, in baskets.

She knew, logically, that with a little thought she could find her way back to the familiar streets, and, if not, she had a tongue in her head and could ask. Why, then, did she feel like an outsider, threatened and unwanted? She stood still, looking around her, trying to rid herself of the uncomfortable sensation that everyone was watching her.

Sudden footsteps sounded on the cobbles behind her, and, before she could turn, there were hands on her shoulders. Hard, dangerous, male hands... Alexandra emitted a little panic-stricken scream and spun round, ready to struggle with her assailant or knee him swiftly in the groin if necessary.

'*Calme-toi!*' Dominic d'Albigny held her forcefully at arm's length, his hands still gripping her shoulders tightly. 'It's only me, you foolish girl—stop thrashing about, or you'll do us both an injury! Whatever are you doing here?'

She might have felt relieved that she was not about to be attacked after all, were it not for the indignity of having to struggle like a fish on a hook.

'Let me go!' she gasped defensively. 'I was just walking—there's no law against it, is there?' She rubbed her shoulders as he released her, annoyed with herself for over-reacting, and avoiding the perceptive amusement in his eyes. 'Why do all these streets look alike? It's like trying to find one's way through a maze!'

'Come, now, there's no way you can get seriously lost in so small an area,' he said scornfully. 'As you can see, many Algerians live in this district. They have their own shops, cafés and customs, and they don't see a lot of tourists. You're probably as safe here as anywhere, but I wouldn't advise any woman to wander aimlessly around a city. It's years since you were in Perpignan, and you are virtually a stranger. Explore, by all means, but get a street map, do it properly and to some purpose.'

Alexandra's irritation was growing by the minute, and she could still feel the imprint of his hands on her. 'Thanks for the lecture,' she said tartly. 'Wasn't I lucky you just happened to be passing by?'

'You surely were, or you might have wandered

around in circles for hours,' he agreed imperturbably. 'Fortunately I often take a short cut this way. And now I suppose I had better escort you back whence you came, before you get lost again.'

Did he have to be this condescending? 'I wasn't really lost, and I can find my own way,' she protested haughtily, but, once his mind was made up, arguing with him did not seem to have any effect. He just ignored her and went right ahead, taking her arm and steering her unerringly through the warren of little streets until they arrived at the Place de la Loge de Mer, a busy square fringed with café tables.

'Have you had breakfast?' he demanded.

Alexandra shook her head mutely. She wanted, and contrarily did not want him to let go of her arm—a thoroughly confusing state of mind. This ever-deepening physical awareness of him made it difficult for her to explain simply that she had fully intended buying bread from the *boulangerie* on her way back from her walk, but had not envisaged being out this long.

He tutted reprovingly at her. 'That's very bad for you.' He pushed her gently but insistently into one of the café chairs, signalled a waiter and ordered coffee, brioches and croissants.

Alexandra glared balefully at him across the table, unsure whether she was angry with him for his high-handedness, or with herself for her lack of resistance.

'Look,' she said, on a rising tide of frustration, 'I'm grateful to you for letting me use your flat, but that doesn't mean you can tell me what and when to eat, where I'm allowed to go, and what I should and should not do!'

He leaned back in his chair, fingers steepled, chin

resting on them, elbows comfortably angled on the chair arms. Her outburst seemed to have had as much effect on him as a fly battering itself against a windscreen.

'Someone should,' he observed equably. 'You don't seem to have too much of an idea yourself. I'm not sure you're even safe to be left on your own. *Alors*, who would have thought you'd grow up into such a feather-brain? You used to be such a clever little thing.'

'Who are you calling a feather-brain?' she demanded, outrage flaring in her eyes. 'It might interest you to know that I have two degrees, the second an MA from Oxford, and I'm presently working for my PhD.'

He inclined his head in acceptance of the information, but, infuriatingly, she could see that it did not alter his opinion one whit.

'So if you have a mind, why don't you use it?' he suggested. 'At the moment you appear to be living on your nerves, which are so close to the surface they are almost visible. You're hardly coming across as a rational, thinking woman.'

'I have feelings as well as intellect, or is that too difficult a concept for you to grasp?' she snapped, stung by the harshness of his tone. If his opinion of her was so low, why did he bother with her at all? she wondered. 'If you must know, someone. . .someone close to me died, and I've been under a bit of a strain.'

If she had expected a sympathetic reaction, she was due for a disappointment. He watched her keenly, but his eyes did not soften. 'This. . ."someone". . . I presume it was a man?'

'I don't want to talk about it,' she said, tight-lipped,

hating the cynicism in his voice and his eyes, which seemed deliberately to mock her grief.

'You don't? Well, I'm certainly not going to force you,' he said in a light, easy tone. 'Ah. . .here are your brioches. Eat them up, then you can decide on a full stomach whether or not you want to go into a decline.'

Alexandra jumped up, shaking with indignation, but he was quicker. Placing a hand on each of her chair's arms, virtually forcing her to subside back into her seat, he leaned over, his face very close to hers as if he were about to kiss her. No one took the slightest notice of them—such things were commonplace. Alexandra felt trapped and helpless, but her breathing was ragged as she gazed up, mesmerised, into his eyes, convinced that at any moment his mouth would touch hers, and unable to persuade herself that she did not want this to happen.

She felt the warmth of his breath on her cheek, and involuntarily her eyes half closed, waiting, wondering why she was so strongly affected by this man who was almost a stranger to her, whose motives she did not understand. But when he spoke she was jerked out of her trance and back into shocked alertness.

'Now,' he said, his voice soft with menace but looking to all outward appearances like a man whispering sweet nothings into a girl's ear, 'tell me why you really came back here, if not to stir up trouble.'

Hot shame flooded Alexandra's face, and she told herself firmly that *of course* she had not wanted him to kiss her—the idea was ridiculous! Why should she tell him, she thought mutinously, that she had come back because here, and only here, she had thought she had family who would hold out a hand for her to grasp when she needed it most? She wasn't going to plead for his sympathy, or throw her loneliness at his feet.

'If you're so clever, you can work that out for yourself,' she said. 'Come to that, who are you to prevent me seeing anyone I choose to see? What about your brother, Michel—he was a lot of fun, I remember. Would he turn me away? And Sabine and Danielle— we all got on well, as girls.'

'My brother lives at Château Albigny, and whatever he thinks privately he will abide by the ground rules,' he said brusquely. 'My sisters are both married with children of their own, but when the head of this family makes a decision the other members will close ranks and stand by it.'

He had resumed his seat, but still had her fixed in his sights. Alexandra refused to be unnerved by the hypnotic quality of his gaze. She fought back hard, and leaned forward triumphantly, carrying the battle to him.

'But you are not the head of your family, and neither is Tante Corinne. Your father is Comte d'Albigny, is he not?'

A grim, saturnine smile lit his face, sending shivers down her back. 'My father died two years ago,' he said. 'Didn't you register what the concierge called me, yesterday: "Monsieur le Comte". Not that I use the title. I'm plain Dominic d'Albigny in most of my dealings, but it still means a lot to people of the older generation. And it *does* make me head of the family.'

It seemed to Alexandra that he watched her very closely, studying her reaction to this information. But Alexandra had never been especially fond of Oncle Matthieu. He had had a plentiful supply of ready charm, but beneath it she had always sensed a shallowness, a lack of purpose and direction. She had thought that Dominic's mother, Tante Françoise, whom she had liked very much, had always looked just a little sad, and certainly her husband had never appeared to pay her much attention.

However, she said, 'I'm sorry to hear that,' because it was the correct thing to say even though, now she came to think of it, Dominic and his father had never got on all that well. 'It must have been painful for your mother.'

He looked hard and directly into her eyes. 'In some ways,' he said. 'You see how out of touch we are with each other, Alexandra? There's nothing here for you any more.'

'So you say. But it seems to me that I have a right to know why I'm being shunned like a leper. You may believe it or not, as you choose, but I truly don't have any idea,' she said.

'Then I should not be the one to tell you,' he insisted firmly. 'So far as I am concerned, the subject is closed. It would be far better for you to forget it, go back to your college and get on with your work. I'm perfectly willing to lend you my apartment for a few more days, so long as I can foresee an end to the arrangement. Let Madame la Concierge know when it will be convenient for you to leave.'

Alexandra found that she was quivering with a rage she could hardly trouble to conceal. Before her on the table the aroma of freshly brewed coffee tantalised her nostrils, the brioches were hot and tempting, and she had eaten nothing. But she would choke, she was convinced, if she had to sit at this table with this hateful, arrogant man, and try to eat.

'You may have your apartment back whenever you wish,' she declared coldly. 'Just let *me* know when you'd like to move back in, and I'll be out like a flash! But I'll go home when I'm good and ready. You may be Comte d'Albigny, but you don't rule Perpignan these days, and you can't have me ridden out of town! You can't force me to leave!'

He endured this tirade without batting an eyelid, and made no move to prevent her when she pushed back her chair and stalked off without a backward glance. She was halfway back to the Castillet before she realised that she was heading back, like a homing piegon, to the safe refuge of the apartment he had just said he wanted her to vacate. As if it were not his home, but hers.

Evening came early at this time of year. Alexandra had made herself a lunch of crusty bread from the *boulangerie*, cheese, tomatoes and coffee, and carried it out on to the sunny balcony where there were cane chairs and tables amid a veritable jungle of plants in tubs. She enjoyed this simple food more than any meal she had eaten in months—eating, like sleeping, had become for her a sporadic 'take it or leave it' business, but anger must have fuelled her appetite today, and she ate heartily.

But her frustration and fury did not noticeably abate. To think that once, as a child, she had been Dominic's fervent little disciple, following him around, hanging on his every word. To think that she had once felt for him all the blind, passionate adoration of a young girl's first love!

They went back a long way, but he wanted nothing more than to send her packing, as if their young lives had never been so closely intertwined—as if she were an annoying stranger who had turned up expressly to cause trouble and embarrassment. He refused to tell her why this should be. He would not unravel for her the puzzle of the past, as only he was in a position to do.

Alexandra sat for a long time on the balcony watching the light fade, the stark black outlines of the mountains standing proud against the blood-red of the setting sun. She would not be sent away like a naughty child who had strayed into a forbidden room. Even if her family would not welcome her, this sun-drenched land between the high Pyrenees and the shining sea held the key to a peace she thought she had lost forever. She felt as if she were in a different world from the one she had left behind, so dark and depressing and full of sad memories. . .

Too much! Alexandra sat bolt upright suddenly as the realisation hit her. For the best part of twenty-four hours she had scarcely thought about Tristan. Well, yes, she had thought about him, even mentioned him indirectly, but she had not grieved.

A wave of guilt assailed her. Of course, she knew she *had* to get over him, she needed to recover herself to the point where she could function normally and carry on with her work. Heaven knew, she had no desire to live all her life in the emotional chaos of the last few months. But to let herself forget, like that, for more than a day... How *could* I? she thought, anguished.

It was *his* fault. Dominic's. She had been so obsessed by this awful, mysterious business at the château, so tied up with memories of the past. Worse—she had to admit it—all her emotions had been knotted up by him, tangled into skeins of anger and misunderstanding, resentment and attraction...

Attraction? No! Alexandra stood up jerkily and went indoors, turning her back on the seductive sky and the pin-pointed lights of the darkening city. She would *not* admit it! It had to be the most utter nonsense. What she felt was no more than the half-forgotten intimations of the girl and boy they had once been.

She bit her lip, recalling that brief, paralysing moment in the car, and that heart-stopping instant at the café when she had thought he was about to kiss her. Resolutely, she pushed those images away. She was not a fifteen-year-old girl now, but a woman, recently bereaved. She called up the memory of Tristan's soulful, haunted face to dispel that of her cousin's hard, aquiline profile, his dark, cynical eyes.

As night fell, she took out the slim folder she had been unable to resist slipping into her suitcase. Get right away from everything, the dean had advised her; clear your mind. But these were Tristan's last poems, written during the time she had known him, and on the night he died she had promised herself she would bring them to light, to the public recognition which might have saved him had he only received it in time.

She carried them over to Dominic's black ash dining-table which stood in an alcoved corner of the salon, and switched on the art-deco pendant lamp so that she sat in a golden pool of light. Spread out before her, they seemed pitifully few for the struggle he'd had to produce them, scribbled on odd scraps of paper, some only half finished, all difficult to read, full of alterations and corrections in Tristan's unintelligible scrawl.

'Well, of course, Miss. . .er. . . Warner,' the flamboyantly trendy young man in the publisher's office had said languidly, 'we did publish Tristan Carteret before, but that was. . .oh. . .fifteen years ago, in my father's time, and he's done nothing significant since. But if you'd like to let me see this work when you've got it into a presentable state. . .'

There was no way she could pick up the threads of her own work until she had fulfilled that promise. Alexandra worked until her eyes ached. At some stage she got up, went into the kitchen, and absent-mindedly cooked herself an omelette, not bothering to wash up afterwards. She poured herself a glass of Dominic's excellent cognac, lit another cigarette and pressed on until she could take no more.

Finally, her head throbbing, she undressed and fell into bed. She would dream about Tristan tonight, she was sure. In what her favourite poet, Rossetti, called 'the speaking silence' of a dream where reality was just beyond one's grasp, she would see his face again. It would hurt. . .it always hurt. . .but it was a bittersweet pain she welcomed.

But the face that floated before her closed eyes was that of her cousin Dominic. Mocking, amused, distrustful, black hair winged back from the faintly scarred temple, a disparaging gleam in the night-dark eyes. 'Here are your brioches. Eat them up, then you can decide on a full stomach whether or not you want to go into a decline. . .' 'Who would have thought you'd grow up into such a feather-brain. . .?' There's nothing here for you any more. . .'

Damn Dominic! Alexandra pummelled the pillow viciously, and turned over, tossing restlessly. She was exhausted, but stretched as taut as a drum, and it was a long, long time before she managed to get to sleep.

And when she did, there were no dreams.

CHAPTER THREE

ALEXANDRA awoke to the unmistakable sound of someone moving about in the apartment, and, in her sleep-drugged state, immediately froze with horror. There was an intruder and she was alone, with no real hope of evading him...and in her nightshirt, moreover!

She slipped out of bed very quietly, her eyes now more accustomed to the room's darkness, casting about her for a weapon. There was none, but if she could only reach the kitchen... She tiptoed barefoot across the vestibule, and just as she reached the kitchen door Dominic emerged from the living-room.

Why hadn't she realised it would be he? Alexandra stopped in her tracks, immobilised by relief and anger, a tall, slim girl in a very short nightshirt—the top button of which had worked itself undone so the garment was half slipping from one shoulder—eyes wide, hair all over the place.

His eyes surveyed her unhurriedly, and she stood as if in a spotlight, exposed to his slow, careful examination.

'*Alors!*' he said appreciatively. 'Cousin Alexandra, if I may say so, you are the owner of a very decent pair of legs—and I am in a position to judge, right now.'

She glared at him, reddening. He was wearing cream chinos and a taupe silk shirt; his immaculate coolness made her feel even more undressed than she was.

'You don't know how close you came to receiving the attentions of a kitchen knife, sneaking in on me like that!' she said accusingly.

'Sneaking?' His eyebrows rose, his eyes moved to the pale, silky skin of her bare shoulder. 'That's odd. I thought I owned this place.'

She shivered involuntarily. He was beginning to make her feel absurdly vulnerable, and she wished she could get some clothes on!

'If you want me out, Dominic, I told you, I'll go!' she snapped. 'You don't have to resort to scare tactics. But so long as I'm here, I'd like some privacy. I don't expect you to walk in at any hour of the day or night.'

'It would be interesting to know exactly what it is that "scares" you,' he remarked obliquely. 'However, if you stopped to think, you'd realise I couldn't phone to tell you I was coming. I unplugged the telephone so that you wouldn't be disturbed. If you don't mind, I'd like to connect it back to the answerphone. It shouldn't bother you too much.'

He favoured her with a knowing grin. 'What do you want to do with all this privacy, anyhow? Entertain scores of lovers?'

Standing in one's nightshirt discussing such things was somehow discomfiting, so Alexandra took refuge in a disdainful silence. He glanced inside the kitchen, and grimaced in distaste.

'Clearly you've been doing nothing so mundane as housekeeping, by the look of it. Don't you ever wash up?'

'Of course I do,' she said, shamefacedly looking away from the unwashed dishes. 'I just happened to be busy.'

He switched on the coffee percolator and marched back into the living-room. Alexandra, recalling the way she had simply left everything when she went to bed last night, was about to forestall him. But she decided that it was better he should see all the mess than that she should continue to follow him about, half clad. She darted back into the bedroom, grabbed her robe and belted it firmly round her waist before hurrying after him. She found him eyeing the dining area with disgust.

'Ugh! What a tip! Will you just look at that ashtray?'

She glanced down guiltily. Had she really smoked so many cigarettes? She must have completely lost track while she was working.

He picked up a glass, revealing a smear on the table's matt black surface. 'Drink my cognac by all means, but use a coaster, Alexandra. That way you won't leave marks. Not exactly domesticated, are you?'

She stared at him indignantly. Not exactly domesticated? The hours she had spent cleaning up after Tristan, cooking nourishing meals to tempt him to eat. Hours she should have spent on her own thesis—not that she had begrudged them, she thought quickly.

'I was just involved in what I was doing,' she said irritably. 'How was I to know you were going to do an inspection tour? I'll clean the place up, this morning.'

He looked down curiously at the scattered papers. 'This is what kept you so busy, I assume? I suppose I shouldn't object, if it's your thesis.'

'It isn't. My thesis is on Rossetti, Barrett Browning and Brontë. This is. . .just something else I'm doing.'

She moved as if to clear up the papers, but he picked up one of the sheets she had neatly transcribed and began to read.

A DREAM TOO SWEET

'I'd rather you didn't do that,' she said hastily, reaching to take it from him. But he moved it just beyond her grasp, a teasing light in his eyes.

'Why not?' he demanded, looking down at her tauntingly. 'Ah—I see why not! These are yours? Cousin Alexandra is a poet! Don't be shy—let me read them. All writers need critics.'

'I'm not...they're not...' she said distractedly, stalking him round the table while he moved, annoyingly, out of her way. 'Dominic—give that back to me! If you must know, those are the unpublished poems of Tristan Carteret. They aren't ready for anyone to read yet.'

'*You've* read them,' he pointed out.

'Yes, but that's different. I'm editing them.' She lunged, grasped, and he moved yet again, with astounding speed, putting the table between them and smiling at her with malicious triumph. 'You shouldn't expect to out-move a squash player, little cousin!' He waved the paper playfully aloft, somehow managing to read it and evade her at the same time. 'Come and get it, then, if you really want it,' he challenged.

Alexandra leaned against the wall, breathless and resentful. She itched to snatch the paper from him, but something in his invitation, although jokingly worded, made her afraid to. He wasn't the boy she had known years ago. He was a man, full grown and dangerous; they were alone, and there was an element of the situation which frightened her and tempted her at the same time. His eyes held hers across the table, fully aware of her reluctance to come closer, and she glimpsed a wicked satisfaction in them.

And then, point made, moral victory scored, he dropped the paper, letting it flutter to the table.

'I've seen enough, anyhow,' he said dismissively. 'Actually, I had no idea that Carteret was still writing. Some of his early work showed promise, but it wasn't fulfilled. If this is an example of his current writing, I wouldn't think it worth your effort. Pretty average stuff, isn't it? The lines ring pleasantly enough, but the content is slight.'

Alexandra gasped with outrage. 'How dare you?' she demanded, trembling with an intensity of emotion which frightened her. 'Tristan Carteret died earlier this year. He struggled to write those poems against sickness and depression—they were his last testament, if you like. Who are you to sit in judgement?'

Comprehension flashed across his face. 'So that's what this is all about?' He gestured disgustedly at the pile of papers, the ashtray overflowing with stub-ends, the general air of unkempt chaos about the place, as if such emotional messiness, such absence of order and self-control were too distasteful for him to contemplate, let alone sympathise with. 'Get the blinkers off, Alexandra. You're an intelligent, educated woman—or so you would have me believe. Use the critical faculties which have brought you this far. I didn't know Carteret was dead, and I'm sorry, but I stand by my opinion, nevertheless. Those poems are mediocre, and deep down you probably know it.'

'Stop it, stop it!' Alexandra cried, hearing the pitch of her own voice rising to hysteria. 'I don't want to listen to this! You don't know what you're talking about!'

She reached blindly, instinctively for a cigarette, but

almost before she saw him move he took it from her hand and squashed it in the ashtray.

'Don't do that. It's bad for you,' he rapped authoritatively. 'You're going to listen to me, whether you want to or not. It's natural to grieve, but it has to end somewhere, Alexandra. It's high time you started to pull yourself together, and you would do it if you stopped wallowing in sentimentality and got on with your life. Your *own* life.'

Alexandra's hands flew to her ears to shut out these harsh words. But he grasped each of her wrists in a cruel grip, forcing them away from her face, pinning her against the wall so that her only possible retaliation was to glare at him resentfully. He had no right to demean Tristan's poetry and pour ice-cold water on the only thing she had left, the memory of her feelings for him.

'Leave me alone! You don't understand!' she screamed at him. 'I loved Tristan. *Loved* him!'

'Loved?' A disdainful scepticism flickered in his eyes. 'Look at you. You're a wreck. You don't sleep or eat regularly, you smoke yourself to death, you go off at a tangent at the slightest provocation. Your nerves are shot to pieces, and I'm willing to bet it wasn't this man's death that has left you this way—it was what he did to you while he was still alive! I'd shoot myself before I'd let a woman get me into such a state!'

'Then you know nothing about love!' she almost spat at him, with bitter satisfaction.

'I know it ruins otherwise perfectly sensible people's lives,' he retorted sharply, and for a moment she saw an intensity of feeling equal to her own twist his features. But only for a moment, then it was gone.

'Give me honest friendship or straightforward lust in preference, every time. Think, Alexandra. What did he ever give *you*, in return for all the time, effort and heartbreak you obviously lavished on him? He made you suffer, isn't that the truth? He's *still* making you suffer, even from beyond the grave.'

She turned her head away but could not escape the conclusive triumph in his voice, or, what was worse, the little, nagging spirit of her own doubts which she fought desperately to suppress, but couldn't—not entirely.

Suffer? Yes, she had suffered, never knowing what she would find if she left the flat for an hour or two: whether he would be full of sullen self-pity, or writhing in pain from the stomach ulcer for which he would not seek treatment. She had become isolated from most of her friends; she had dared not leave Tristan alone too much, and he had found most of them immature and had treated them insultingly. And, along with her constant, gnawing anxiety over him, there had been the worry over how little her own work was progressing.

She'd tried. Oh, she'd tried. But it had grown increasingly difficult. 'Of course,' he had said unpleasantly, waking one evening from a whisky-induced sleep to find her with her books spread over the table, trying to snatch an hour, 'I do realise that your doctoral thesis is infinitely more important than my puny efforts, and will be read long after I'm forgotten.' He hadn't worked for a week after that, and naturally that had been *her* fault.

But he hadn't been in control of those unkind things he had said to her, more frequently as his condition had deteriorated. He had been sick and disillusioned and somehow lost, and she had counted it a privilege to have shared his last months. His poems were a legacy to the world; they *had* to have value, otherwise all she had endured meant very little.

At this thought Alexandra's lower lip began to tremble a little, and she bit hard on it, tasting blood and salt. It hurt, and so did the fierce grip of Dominic's fingers, still pinioning her wrists, but neither were as painful as the cold, analytical searchlight he was forcing her to shine on her own innermost convictions and feelings.

She raised her head slowly, looking into the enigmatic, questioning eyes, and a tremor ran through her, her skin beginning to prickle. Like a cramped limb returning to life, she felt the painful surging of blood through dormant veins. Something old and half buried stirred inside her and turned over, making her stomach lurch and her mouth run dry. Past and present telescoped briefly together, driving all that had happened between out of her mind. She no longer knew whether she was here, in his apartment, or back in the stable with Dominic—it was one and the same. She was aching to be kissed, and more, burning with strange sensations which left her guilty and excited all at once. . .

A deep sigh welled up within her, like a bursting stream, dammed too long. The kiss she had wanted all those years ago was here and now; she forgot Oxford, forgot Tristan, forgot everything but the vibrant, tingling nearness of this man, and the pent-up electricity of her own unbearable anticipation. . .

'"Oh dream how sweet, too sweet, too bitter sweet,"' he quoted softly, drawing her slowly towards him as if impelled by the same irresistible impulse, '"whose wakening should have been in Paradise. . ."'

All vestige of colour drained from the translucent skin of Alexandra's face, leaving her pale, and she began to shake like a leaf in the wind.

'Don't!' she moaned, staring at him, eyes wide with anguish. And then, as she stood there, tears welled up in her eyes and spilled out, tracing rivulets down her cheeks. Since Tristan died, she had been unable to weep properly. The pain had been frozen inside her, as hard and impacted as polar ice. Now she could not stop, she stood there crying like a fool, and the worst of it was that she did not truly know why.

The lines he had spoken were Christina Rossetti's, as he must have been aware she would know, lines full of lost love and sorrow and despair. But what was the dream too sweet—was it the doomed love she had felt for Tristan, or did it go further back, deeper down, to the innocent girl she had once been, and the thwarted infatuation which had cast a shadow over her young life?

Racked by confusion, Alexandra felt the strength drain suddenly from her body. She did not faint or become dizzy; it was simply as if the power of her limbs to support her were switched off at the mains, and she began to crumple and slide to the ground.

But he was there ahead of her, bending swiftly and gathering her up into his arms, carrying her to the nearest sofa where he sat cradling her as if she were a child. Great sobs tore her throat, and she turned her face instinctively against the taupe silk shirt, and the steady reassuring beat of his heart beneath it, her tears making a slowly spreading damp patch.

'*Pauvre petite*, go on, cry,' she heard him murmur through the storm of her own emotions. Then he said no more, just held her, letting her weep until there were no tears left, and her sobs quietened of their own accord.

One arm still round her shoulders, he reached for a box of king-sized tissues from the table by the sofa. 'Mop up, before we both drown,' he said, not unkindly.

Alexandra seized a handful and scrabbled at her damp, reddened face. His hand was warm on her shoulder through the thin stuff of her robe, the tanned face was very close to her own. Embarrassed by her own weakness, more disturbed by his nearness than she cared to admit, she searched his face for any sign of mockery or amusement, and for once, astonishingly, found none.

'What an idiot I am,' she said in a low voice. 'Losing control of myself like that. You must think me quite mad.'

'*Pas du tout*,' he said politely. 'There is no shame in tears—that is a very English inhibition. Perhaps you needed to cry. It's the first step in the healing process.'

Perhaps—if it had been, as he was assuming, a straightforward release of grief. But Alexandra knew, deep down, that her feelings were far more complex than that. Even now, she hardly dared admit to herself how much her awakening memories and her fierce, disturbing present-day response to him were to blame. She looked into his eyes, searchingly, as if pleading for an answer only he could give her, and for a moment he continued to hold her. The air around them trembled with possibilities, as if one of them need only make the slightest move for the situation to spill over into passion.

Then he said gently, 'I think I had better let you go, *ma chérie*,' and shamefacedly she scrambled off his lap, telling herself that the fraught atmosphere existed only in her imagination. He had comforted her as he might a crying child, with a tenderness and sensitivity she had not suspected he could show towards her. But that was all, and she had to conclude that he was not moved by having her in his arms. After all, he never had been.

She stood, arms clasped, hugging herself tightly. 'Why did you do that?' she demanded reproachfully. 'What made you quote those particular lines? What were you trying to do?'

He shrugged expressively. 'They came to my mind,' he said, a trifle evasively. 'They're from a poem called "Echoe", a lament for a lost lover. Perhaps I thought it would strike a chord. You're too bottled up, Alexandra. You need, and you *want*—whatever you might say to the contrary—to let some of it out.'

She had thought the words were especially for her, a way of showing her that he remembered the past, and that it had some meaning for him, too. But it seemed it had been no more than a deliberate manipulation of her emotions.

'Playing amateur psychiatrist, were we?' she demanded huffily. 'Well, kindly don't bother. I'll get over my grief in my own way—and at my own speed.'

And now the tenderness and concern were gone from his eyes as surely as if they had never been there, so that she thought she must have imagined them, too.

'You'll only *allow* yourself to get over it when you

accept certain truths,' he said with cool scorn. 'It's easier to cling to illusions than to shed them.'

He unwound his tall, limber frame easily from the sofa and pointed to the pile of papers on the table. 'Start with those. Who knows where it might lead you?'

'Go away!' she said in a low, choked voice. 'I don't care what you say or what you think. I loved Tristan—as he loved me—and I'm going to see that his last works are published. Nothing else matters to me.'

Beyond a slight arching of the eyebrows, he showed no visible response to this outburst. '*D'accord*. As you wish,' he said, and picking up her cigarettes he slipped them into his pocket. 'But I'll take these. Oh, I know it's a fairly pointless gesture. The *tabac* across the road won't have run out. But if it makes you think twice before you light up, it won't have been entirely in vain.'

Alexandra longed to pick up the heavy glass and onyx ashtray and hurl it at the door as it closed behind him. Who was he to stride in here and set about diminishing everything she cared for? Standing there in the prime of life and health, with the unassailable background of his secure, ancient inheritance, good looks, money and success, all life's advantages handed to him on a plate, pouring contempt on her love for Tristan, his love for her. Criticising work he was in no position to judge—why, English was not even his mother tongue!

She frowned, and gave an impatient little shake of the head, as if she would dispel from her mind whatever did not suit her argument. But a few traumatic, abandoned months could not so easily overcome years of disciplined thought. Both the d'Albigny boys, Dominic and Michel, had been educated at a well-known English public school, as had generations of d'Albignys before them. Dominic's English was up to any test, and his mental powers too sharp for his own good.

She shuffled the papers back into the folder and closed it firmly. She could not bear to reread them, not now. Of course, she'd read them many times before, but with a mind too clouded by emotion to see beyond her own committed purpose. She dared not, at this moment, look further than the pleasing technical arrangement of metre and metaphor, for fear of discovering what Dominic had condemned as 'slight'.

For what if he was right. . .even in part? What else might he not be right about? He had advised her to shed a few illusions and see where it might lead her.

Might it not lead her to wondering, just a little, just occasionally, if her love for Tristan had been no more than the unhealthy obsession of a lonely young woman, not worldly enough to know that she was being used? If his for her had been only the need for a good brain, a female body, and a willing pair of hands?

Alexandra fought like the devil to close her mind to these doubts and questionings, but something strange had happened to her during these few days in France. She was emerging, gradually and painfully, from the cocoon in which she had been wrapped for so long, and the newly exposed surfaces were tender and untried.

She got up swiftly, went into the black, sybaritic bathroom, and stripped off her robe and nightshirt, tossing them on to the floor. Her naked reflection stared back at her from the mirror, and briefly she stood there, taking stock of it, trying to be objective.

Christine Warner had unquestionably been a beautiful woman, and, like many daughters of beautiful women, Alexandra had never thought of herself as pretty by comparison. Her hair was the same red-gold, but where Christine's had fallen into easy, natural waves her own was thick, straight and unmanageable. Her face was too angular, lacking her mother's regularity of feature.

'It's a good thing that girl has brains,' she had once heard a friend of her mother's remark, and she had been hurt, but resigned. As an adolescent she had been skinny and underdeveloped, too much height and not enough flesh. But the beanpole effect had halted itself, leaving her a slender five feet eight. Her legs were long and slim, and amazingly, in spite of the years when she had thought despairingly that nothing was going to happen, she had good breasts.

She turned on the shower briskly, and stepped under it. Why this sudden, excessive interest in her own body? She had never thought much about it before. She had gone to Tristan virtually untouched, innocent for her years, and he had taken her swiftly, sometimes a little too roughly, clinging to her for comfort in the night. Sometimes she had wondered guiltily if there might not be more, then she had stifled such disloyal, selfish thoughts. To give where she was needed should surely be enough?

Dominic certainly did not need her. He did not even want her. To him she was a nuisance, an argumentative, slightly neurotic female who had taken over his apartment, threw hysterical tantrums every time they met—and she was sure he'd be glad to see the back of her.

And yet. . .all the same, when he touched her, she found herself at the mercy of unknown sensations. The searing memory of that kiss they had nearly shared, long ago, the certainty of what would have followed had their lips touched, haunted her like a dream from which she had been rudely awoken at the sweetest moment. She had lived that dream again, briefly, today.

How could a woman who had lost the man she loved not six months earlier have thoughts like this about any man? It was wrong. It was indecent. She had been touched by the sun. She was going off her head.

What other explanation could there be?

CHAPTER FOUR

FOR the next two days, Alexandra had the apartment to herself, undisturbed by any visits or even any word from Dominic. But his influence reached out and touched her, none the less.

Determined to refute his accusation that she could not look after herself and didn't eat properly, she shopped and cooked, finding interesting ingredients in the local markets and making use of the variety of cookery books on his shelves.

Anxious to prove that she was not weak-willed and helpless, she stopped smoking, and almost at once everything she ate tasted fresher, more flavoursome. Not that it was easy—she averted her eyes from the rows of cigarette packs in the *tabac* when she bought her newspaper, and marched out congratulating herself for not succumbing.

Tristan's poems, however, remained untouched in their folder. That was a test she was not yet ready to face. She submerged herself instead in trivial domestic tasks, watering Dominic's many plants and polishing every surface in the apartment until it shone. And, the next morning, his cleaning lady turned up.

Her name was Marthe, she was plump, middle-aged and indefatigable, and had obviously been briefed by *madame la concierge* about Alexandra's existence. Treating Alexandra's efforts as negligible, she huffed and puffed around the place doing everything again and to her own satisfaction, and while thus occupied she talked—incessantly.

Was Alexandra, then, the granddaughter of Mademoiselle Antoinette who had run off with that British officer? Was she married, had she any children? She was still at university—at her age? Studying for a doctorate? *Tiens*, the things girls did these days!

Alexandra answered all her questions patiently and then thought, Right, I've satisfied her curiosity, surely I'm entitled to ask a few questions of my own?

She said, 'I'm afraid I'm not too welcome up at the château, because of what happened last time I was here. It was a long time ago, but perhaps you can remember.'

Marthe might never have worked at the château, but servants gossiped, and Alexandra gambled on her having heard something from someone. Sure enough, she saw an instant reaction in the other woman's eyes; she paused for a moment in her vigorous polishing, and Alexandra thought she looked embarrassed, uncomfortable.

'Oh, *that*,' Marthe said, and then, hastily correcting herself, 'Well, I did hear there was something, some carry-on, but I'm sure I don't know what it was all about.'

Alexandra was equally sure she did, but clearly Marthe valued her job and wasn't going to discuss any scandal in her employer's family. There appeared to be nothing to be gained by pumping her further on that subject, so she ventured casually, 'Have you worked for Monsieur Dominic for very long?'

'Oh. . .let me see. . .it must be almost four years, ever since he took this place,' Marthe said cheerfully.

'He's particular, is Monsieur le Comte, likes things just so, and I'm thorough, so I suit him.'

'I can see you are,' Alexandra agreed. 'It's a very attractive apartment. . .for a bachelor, that is. It wouldn't be very practical for a family. But then, my cousin hasn't married.'

'*Mais non!* He's still a young man, only thirty,' Marthe protested. 'A man must first enjoy himself, no? It is understood. Especially a man like Monsieur le Comte. When he does marry, it will have to be someone suitable—for the family, for the château, you know.'

It had not actually occurred to Alexandra until that moment that, even today, aristocratic old families like the d'Albignys did not marry simply for love, but took care to choose someone 'suitable'. Someone rich, perhaps, but even more importantly someone with the right background and social connections. And, until he decided to settle down with that person, Dominic would presumably feel as free as his ancestors had felt to sample as many women as suited him. . .on the basis that they amused or attracted him, but must never presume they might one day become Comtesse d'Albigny.

How feudal, she thought—the lord of the manor exercising his *droit du seigneur* among the peasantry until the chosen virgin was selected! Her mother had been right—the Warners were poor relations who had nothing in common with that way of life. . .only it had never seemed so, when they were young. For all she had been aware they had money and property, she had never been made to feel that there was any difference between herself and the young d'Abignys. A pang of nostalgia for the simplicity of those days shook her, and she was aware of a deep sadness that it could never be recaptured.

After Marthe had gone, she was restless and could settle to nothing. It was her own fault—talking about Dominic had brought him to the forefront of her mind again. Not that he was ever far from it, she thought wretchedly.

She decided to divert herself with a little sightseeing, and walked through the city to the Palace of the Kings of Majorca, from where, in the Middle Ages, the Catalan kingdom had been ruled. It was just as she remembered it. The view from the top of the ramparts, blood-red in the sun, was out of this world—clear to the shining horizon of the sea in one direction, across the Plain of Roussillon to the Corbiéres and the Pyrenees in the other.

Dominic's ancestors must have trodden these very halls as courtiers of those kings. Catalans themselves by origin, not Frenchmen, their blood-lines linked with those of their kinsmen across the frontier in Spain, and the family had a long and chequered history.

And now she was thinking about him again! It seemed that, the more time passed without any contact between them, the more he invaded her thoughts. Perhaps she could only free herself from this growing preoccupation by confronting him. Only then could she persuade herself that these strange feelings were no more than lingering echoes of her girlish obsession. . .that she did not want his touch, his kisses, or any part of him.

The conviction grew until it was impossible to ignore it. She had to see Dominic. But how, if she was not allowed to contact Château Albigny, and he seemed to have forgotten her existence? Alexandra walked slowly back to the apartment, and only as she entered the lobby did an idea strike her.

'*Madame.*' She approached the concierge, who looked up from her knitting, behind her desk.

'*Mademoiselle?*' She had watched Alexandra's comings and goings with a keen eye, but they had exchanged no more than polite comments about the weather so far.

'*Madame*. . . I need to get in touch with my cousin, but. . .when he is not at the château, I wonder if there is anywhere else I might be able to contact him?'

Perhaps, she hoped, Dominic had a favourite café or restaurant where he could frequently be found, or a message left for him? Concierges were notoriously mines of such information—if they wanted to part with it.

The woman eyed her carefully, weighing up her request. 'If he is not at the château, he will most probably be at Roussillon Village,' she said. 'Have you tried there?'

'I don't know where it is,' Alexandra confessed. Or even *what* it was. But she wasn't going to admit this much ignorance of Dominic's lifestyle. The concierge presumably knew as much as Marthe did about Alexandra's status with regard to the château, but, she hoped, nothing at all about matters between Dominic and herself on a personal level. Hopefully, she would think that since Alexandra was staying in his apartment he was amicably disposed towards her.

She must have assumed so. 'You have to go out along the Canet-Plage road, turn off through old Canet village, keep going a little way, and it is on your right,' she informed her.

Alexandra thanked her and walked briskly along to the Promenad des Platanes to investigate the bus service. The bus, she found, would take her to Canet or to the beach resort of Canet-Plage, but not, the official told her, along the road past Roussillon Village.

Alexandra frowned. '*Que-est-ce-que c'est*, Roussillon Village?' she asked. 'What exactly is it?'

The official looked at her as if she were an idiot. She wanted to go to Roussillon Village, but she had no idea what she would find when she got there? 'It's a *village de vacances, mademoiselle*. What else?'

A holiday complex? What in the world was Dominic likely to be doing there? Playing squash, perhaps? Relaxing in the jacuzzi? He certainly would not welcome her appearance, she thought ruefully, but no matter. By now, this had become a riddle Alexandra had to solve. She abandoned the idea of the bus, and went back to the car-hire company.

Driving along the road which led towards the coast, she was amazed by the amount of new building that was going on all around. Holiday developments, flats, new housing of all kinds—even the road itself was in the process of being enlarged at several points. She remembered it as a sleepy area of small resorts that only the French—and not so many of them—knew about, surrounded by farms and vineyards. Now it was booming with development.

Turning off the main road, she found the old village of Canet, thankfully much as she remembered it with its small square and gardens, and the *mairie* occupying a central position flanked by two streets of shops—the *boulangerie*, the *poissonerie*, a couple of bars. And beyond the village the road was quiet and rural, fringed by trees and fields of vines. There couldn't be a *village de vacances* here!

She almost missed it, driving past what looked like someone's country estate. Only a discreet sign, 'Roussillon Village', above a white stuccoed archway alerted her, and just in time she turned down a cool, tree-shaded drive to a parking area.

Alexandra pulled up, switched off the engine, and got out. Beyond this point, everything was pedestrianised. Narrow pathways wound between small blocks of villas and apartments, none more than three storeys high. Some were washed pink, others beige, or white, or cream; each was somehow individual, with doors, shutters, roof-tiling and wrought-iron stairways subtly different from its neighbours, yet blending into a harmonious whole. Gardens surrounded it, brilliant with roses, violas, geraniums and a proliferation of scented shrubs and trees. A small stream, criss-crossed by bridges, snaked its way between the buildings, lending a faintly Venetian ambience.

She emerged on to a central plaza. There was a large L-shaped pool surrounded by palm trees and a terrace with sun-loungers. A handful of people were swimming, others drinking in a pleasant bar, partly open to the sky. The clink of glasses and cutlery advertised the proximity of a restaurant.

Alexandra hesitated, looking around her. Roussillon Village was a delightful place, but where would she find Dominic—if indeed he was here? The concierge had sounded certain that he would be, but she could see no sign of him and was beginning to have second thoughts about this mad venture.

He would not want to see her. If he did, he knew where to find her and could easily have done so. If this was indeed somewhere he came to unwind, he would be very angry with her for invading his privacy, and Dominic, angry, was a phenomenon to avoid, she thought with a reminiscent shudder.

She was about to turn tail and head back to the car when a slim, elegant blonde woman in her thirties emerged from the reception office.

'Can I help you, *mademoiselle*?' she asked. 'Are you perhaps looking for someone?'

Alexandra wondered if it was still possible or advisable to retreat, then she squared her shoulders and took a deep breath. Did she want to see him, or didn't she? He couldn't bite her, could he? She wasn't afraid of him.

'Actually, yes,' she said. 'I was told I would find Monsieur le Comte d'Albigny here.'

She thought there was a touch of amusement in the other woman's smile. 'The Comte...ah, you mean Dominic,' she said, and Alexandra recalled him saying that he did not use the title. 'Yes, he's here, somewhere. I could find him for you if you don't mind waiting.'

'Perhaps it's inconvenient,' Alexandra began doubtfully.

'Not at all. Please come this way.' She led Alexandra to the bar, installed her at a table in a nicely secluded corner with a view of the pool, and signalled to the young man behind the bar. 'Jean-Louis will look after you. Who shall I say is asking for Dominic?'

'His cousin, Alexandra Warner.'

She thought a look of interest flickered between the other two at this information, but perhaps she only imagined it, then the blonde woman hurried away.

'Can I get you a drink, Miss Warner?' the young man called Jean-Louis asked politely in English. He brought the lemonade she asked for, and smiled with shy delight when she complimented him on his English.

'All the properties here are privately owned, and many of the owners are English,' he explained. 'Therefore it is necessary for the staff to speak both languages. Not all your compatriots are as fluent in French as you are, *mademoiselle*.'

Not all my compatriots have had the opportunity to learn the way I did, she thought, but she accepted the compliment graciously. Did Dominic own a villa here? Why should he, when he had an apartment in Perpignan and the château only a few miles away?

Unless. . .she went ice-cold with horror as the thought struck her. . .unless he maintained one as a discreet hide-out for his current lady-friend—one of those women who accepted that they could only be a plaything, not a serious candidate for the role of Comtesse d'Albigny.

She sat rooted to her chair, appalled by her own impulsive stupidity in coming here. It was sheer lunacy! But Madame la Concierge had cheerfully given her directions, and neither Jean-Louis nor the blonde woman from reception seemed perturbed by her arrival. Could it be that the French truly did have a different, more relaxed attitude towards such things?

Please, lord, let him simply be playing squash, she prayed. She had spent two days fantasising unwillingly about his touch, the warmth of his arms when he'd held her, the curve of his mouth close to hers. Had she come in wild search of a man who was making love to another woman right now? Had she learned nothing since she was fifteen—not even to keep away from where she was not wanted?

'Alexandra? Is there a problem?'

She was so engrossed in her own horrific ramblings that she did not hear him approach. Her heart gave an apprehensive lurch as she looked up to see him regarding her questioningly.

He wore black trousers and a crisp, short-sleeved white shirt, every hair on his head was immaculately in place, he looked groomed, businesslike, his eyes sharp, his manner alert. Not a man interrupted from a romantic rendezvous, she thought with relief. But he hardly looked as if he had been playing squash, either.

'Not really.' She had concocted during the drive out an excuse for coming to see him, but it sounded limp and implausible now. 'Only—you never did say how long I could occupy your apartment. I need to know, so that I can plan accordingly.'

He looked more than a little sceptical. 'Are you thinking of going home soon, then?'

There was something about his readiness to pack her off back to England that Alexandra found hurtful. Did the past count for nothing, and was she now no more than an inconvenience, a blip on the graph of a life that ran smoothly without her?

'I told you, I'm not going to leave Perpignan simply because it suits you that I should,' she retorted defensively. 'But I might need to look for somewhere else to stay.'

He gave a snort of disbelief, and his stare was so penetrating that she had to look away.

'If you're going to lie, Alexandra, learn to do it more convincingly. Otherwise, if your motivation in coming here was sheer female curiosity, admit it! I suppose Madame la Concierge told you where you would find me. *Bien*, it's not a secret. But be honest about it.'

Alexandra only wished her motivation were that simple. But better he should think her merely inquisitive than guess at the complicated tangle of her true feelings. She was saved from replying by the blonde woman from the office, who interrupted them apologetically.

'Excuse me, Dominic, but Monsieur Lebecq is on the telephone from Switzerland. I told him you were occupied, but nothing will satisfy him but to speak to you personally.'

'Very well, Chantal. Tell him I'll be a minute. And while you're in the office fax through those details to Paris, will you?'

Alexandra frowned. There could be no mistaking that this was a business conversation, and she turned from Chantal's retreating back to look up at Dominic, puzzled at first, until the pieces clicked into place in her mind. 'Dominic. . . Roussillon Village belongs to you, doesn't it?'

It was his turn to look puzzled. '*D'accord*,' he said. 'Didn't *madame* also tell you that? What did you think—that I was tucked up in bed here with a *petite amie*?'

This was so close to her actual thoughts that Alexandra flushed scarlet. He laughed softly.

'I have to disappoint you. Reality is much more

prosaic, and I must now go and talk to a very staid Swiss banker. Jean-Louis!' He waved the barman over. 'Bring Miss Warner another drink, and don't let her escape.'

It was said lightly, but there was an ominous note beneath the levity, and his laughter had made her considerably uncomfortable. She hoped he did not want to probe deeper into her reasons for seeking him out. Female curiosity was the most she was prepared to admit to. 'I came here to prove to myself that I'm not really intrigued by or attracted to you' was not a crime to which she dared plead guilty.

Jean-Louis brought her another lemonade and chatted to her about his work, which he obviously enjoyed. He was not always behind the bar, he told her; sometimes he managed the restaurant, sometimes he was in Reception or in the office.

'I learn the management,' he said, 'from a hard but very good teacher.'

There was affectionate admiration as well as respect in his voice, and Alexandra said, 'I would never have expected to find the d'Albignys running this kind of business.'

He gave her a strange look. 'But of course, they don't,' he said. 'They never did. This is purely and simply Dominic's. Creating an exclusive development such as this required a lot of money and a lot of faith, but the old Comte did not put up one franc towards it. Moreover, he let it be known among the local banking fraternity that, if it failed, he could not be relied upon to come to the rescue. Dominic had to arrange the finance for himself, just as you or I would have to do.'

Alexandra blinked. 'Dominic's father did that? But why?'

'It's not really for me to say, Miss Warner.' Again, that loyal discretion made the young man check his tongue. However, he could not resist adding, 'To be sure, the château's finances were very run down by then. There probably wasn't anything to spare, had he wanted to help. When Dominic took over, it was touch and go whether the vineyards would survive. He ran himself to a shadow for a year or so, trying to get them back into profit, overseeing this place at the same time. I don't know how he succeeded in staying sane.'

Behind them, a quiet voice said, 'When you have finished making me sound like Superman, Jean-Louis, you have customers waiting. Miss Warner will never believe I work for a living, anyhow. She thinks I'm a profligate playboy.'

Jean-Louis blushed and hurried away, and Alexandra looked into Dominic's tauntingly smiling face with a shiver of apprehension.

'What are you up to?' he asked in a voice that was deceptively soft, but chilling. 'Asking so many questions of everyone—my cleaning lady, the concierge, my staff here—yes, I know. Why do you need this information?'

'You said it yourself—female curiosity,' she quipped defensively. 'After all, you've told me next to nothing.' Then, deciding that victory favoured the attacker, she went on, 'One might wonder why you decided to go into building development when the vineyards were doing so badly. Why you didn't devote yourself to them at the time.'

'Because, my nosy little cousin, I wasn't offered that

alternative,' he said caustically. 'I had lots of ideas about how to improve the vineyards, but my father wouldn't listen to any of them. The way things had always been done, since the Middle Ages—that was the way they must remain. Not only in the fields, but in commercial practice, too. You would have thought that modern business methods had not been invented.'

His voice was terse and angry, and suddenly he checked himself, casting an accusing look at her as if she were to blame for the way he had spoken.

'Damn! I still feel guilty criticising him, even now. Especially now.'

'I thought you specialised in speaking ill of the dead,' she could not resist interpolating silkily. 'You certainly didn't spare Tristan, for all you didn't know him.'

'I didn't have to know him. I could deduce enough from what *you* said, from the state you were in—just from *looking* at you,' he retorted combatively. 'People don't suddenly become right, become cleverer or more virtuous, in retrospect, simply by virtue of being dead. The fact that my father and I didn't get on isn't relevant. I was right, and I knew it. But he told me if I wasn't prepared to accept his decisions without questions, I could get out. So I did.'

Alexandra caught her breath at this bold statement. Before her eyes, the image of the wealthy, titled youth, born with the proverbial silver spoon, was disintegrating fast, leaving instead a reality that was quite different. A young man estranged from his father, making his own way in the world against parental opposition. She began to see how such a man might have grown hard and cynical, even slightly bitter, in those circumstances.

'Didn't you go home at all, during that time?'

'Only as an occasional visitor. The quarrel was between my father and myself—it was not fair to make my mother, my grandmother, my sisters and brother, suffer unduly. But the visits were somewhat strained.' He forced a smile. 'Also, although I suspected that the vineyards were going rapidly downhill, I had no way of ascertaining the full extent. It came as a shock when I inherited.'

He stopped suddenly, and they looked at each other, each as surprised as the other to find that they had been talking calmly and unemotionally for some minutes. Their eyes remained locked, and in that moment Alexandra felt the rancour and unexplained bitterness which had marred all their meetings draining away. She held her breath at the stunning prospect of a genuine, open and warm relationship developing between them, and it seemed that she had never wanted anything quite so fiercely.

But perhaps this step was not quite so easy or so desirable for him, for he shrugged and said facetiously, 'End of story. Curtain falls on prospering business ventures and son and heir making good. Let's go and have lunch.'

'You don't have to buy me lunch,' she said, plunged into disappointment and feeling that a vital chance had been lost, because he had chosen to turn away from it. What was it that held him back, made him determined to distrust her?

'I know I don't *have* to. But it's lunchtime. I'm hungry. Aren't you?' He helped her to her feet, his hand lingering only briefly under her elbow, his eyes avoiding hers now, deliberately eschewing closeness.

She could have left, then; perhaps, she thought sadly, she should have done so. But she could not bring herself to go. The moment of warmth had existed, briefly—perhaps it would be possible to rekindle it?

In the restaurant, wine glasses sparkled against pristine white napery and dark oak tables, and a vine grew profusely among the rafters and across the white-painted wall. But the star of the show was outside, and Dominic led her to a table by the window with a flourish, as if he had stage-managed it himself. Away in the distance but closer than she had yet seen it, the snow-streaked summit of Mount Canigou, the loftiest peak on this stretch of the mighty Pyrenees, floated serene and majestic, like a great galleon anchored halfway to heaven.

'Oh, my!' she breathed. 'Do you ever get to the stage where you can take that for granted?'

'Never quite,' he admitted. 'You might think that at well over nine thousand feet Canigou would be inescapable, but there are cloudy days, or times when you can't see the mountains for heat haze. Then a clear day comes and Canigou is looking over your shoulder, like a giant, and your breath is taken anew. In winter, of course, it's quite easy to drive up into the mountains for a weekend's skiing. Do you ski, Alexandra?'

A crazy impulse to recapture the closeness they had almost achieved earlier prompted her to say experimentally, 'That's one skill you never taught me.'

His eyes held hers, and for a long heartbeat she saw the past mirrored in his face. 'You were never here in the winter, or I would have. I made quite a good rider of you, though.'

Now it seemed as if her breath were being forced

thickly through cotton wool. The rides through the pine-scented hills, with the sun hot on their backs, his muscular young thigh brushing hers as they rode side by side along the narrow trails. Stopping to eat picnic lunches in the stillness of a mountain clearing, drinking icy water from a stream. Waiting for him to kiss her, not knowing how to let him know she wanted him to. . .

'You wouldn't let me ride Dauphin,' she said, smiling reproachfully. 'You said he was too much horse for a bit of a girl.'

'So I did, but that didn't deter you. You took him out anyway, and I had to come after you. That last day——' He broke off, but his eyes didn't leave her face. The clatter of cutlery, the soft laughter of other diners was as distant as the moon, and they were alone in their capsule of memory. He remembered! She could see that he remembered. . .

'Of all the dangerous, stupid, immature. . .if you ever do that again, Lexi, I'll. . .'

'You'll what, Dominic? I rode him, didn't I? That should prove I'm not a bit of a girl, and I'm not immature. . .'

Sliding from Dauphin's back, and almost into Dominic's arms, she saw his angry, anxious young face close to hers, and her lips parted invitingly. She'd scared him, shaken him deliberately. Anything to make him react, to make him aware of her. . .

She saw his smile for once reach his eyes as he said, almost invitingly, 'Do you still ride, Alexandra?'

'I haven't done too much, lately,' she admitted,

without thinking before choosing her words. 'Tristan didn't——' She bit off the end of the sentence, but it was too late, the capsule was shattered. The present reclaimed them.

'Oh, Tristan,' he said, with a dismissive shrug. 'That's all one ever hears from you. *Tiens!* Alexandra, did you always have to go along with what *he* wanted?'

'It wasn't like that,' she protested fiercely. 'His health wasn't good.' She closed her mind to the memory of his mildly derisive voice declaiming that most sporting activities were mere games for children who had nothing better to do.

'I can imagine,' Dominic said crisply. 'I suppose he was the one who taught you to poison yourself with nicotine.'

'I've stopped smoking,' she said shortly.

'It's a start,' he acknowledged. 'The next step is to recognise your own worth, get on with your thesis. . .sit *down*, Alexandra! You can't keep jumping up and running away every time I say something you don't like.'

His voice was quiet, but dangerously commanding. Alexandra sank back into her chair, her eyes smouldering with banked-up emotion. She was still shaking from the aftermath of the poignant moment when the past had reached out and touched them; her nervous system could not take any more of this kind of overload. But he seemed determined not to spare her.

'This. . . Tristan. You say you loved him. Did you live with him?'

She hesitated, disturbed by the directness of the question, but determined not to avoid answering as honestly as she could. The truth seemed suddenly crucial.

'In a way. I kept my own flat, so I suppose in that sense the answer is "no". But. . .well, I couldn't leave him on his own too much. He was ill, and——'

'I see.' He appeared to be concentrating hard on the blank whiteness of the tablecloth. 'You were a combination of nurse, lover, muse and head-cook-and-bottle-washer? Right?'

She listened hard for the ring of scorn in his voice which so far had never failed to appear whenever this subject arose, but, oddly, it was absent. Instead, there was a disconcerting note of compassion. 'No wonder you were ragged at the edges. What was it that finally killed him?'

Somehow, she found she did not resent the question. 'Peritonitis. A perforated ulcer,' she said. 'He . . . I had to go out, to see my tutor. When I got back, he was in the most awful pain. I called an ambulance, had him admitted to hospital, but things had already gone too far.'

Now she had started talking about it, she found herself unable to stop. Once, she would have thought him the unlikeliest of confidants, but he was listening to her quietly and intently now, as she had listened when he told her of the split with his father.

'I sat all night at the hospital while they performed an emergency operation, but it was no use. Then, at the funeral, his ex-wife turned up.' A spasm of trembling shook her. 'It was dreadful. She was so bitchy, as if it were my fault—their breaking up, his death, everything. But they were divorced long before I met him. I did my best to help him. . . I truly did.'

Dominic's hand reached across the table and covered hers. A slim, elegant hand, but reassuringly strong and firm. 'Alexandra. Stop tormenting yourself. It sounds as if you gave all you had, and then some. He probably had self-destruction programmed into him, and there was nothing you could have done to prevent it. It's over now. Let it go.'

Unconsciously, she had curled her fingers round his in a tight grip. Only when she felt the pressure returned did she realise that she was clinging to his hand. By then she did not want to let go, to break the physical and mystical contact that bound them together.

He'd touched her hand to comfort her, and she had hung on as to a lifeline, but subtly the feeling had changed with her awareness of the warm, hard male fingers. It was no longer reassurance, but an electric tingle of excitement which would not be confined to any one part of her. It leap-frogged crazily up her arm, activating wires all over her body, leaving her legs a limp, useless jelly, while her breasts were unbearably taut.

Not a word was said, but for a brief, subliminal instant a message flashed across her consciousness direct from his. To hell with lunch, it said, let's go somewhere we can be alone and I can make love to you. It was as clear and unmistakable as if he had spoken out loud, and she looked up at him across the table, her heart thumping, her stomach churning, all her responses screaming yes, yes, *yes*!

But the eyes that met hers were unreadable, and she sought in vain for any confirmation there. Slowly, carefully, he uncurled her limpet-like fingers from his and released her hand—a calm and deliberate withdrawal.

'Let's order now, shall we?' was all he said.

How could she have been so mistaken? But it's not the first time, a sober little voice whispered inside her head. You thought he wanted you once before. Remember? It was no more than wishful thinking then. That's all it is now, so don't go making a fool of yourself all over again.

Alexandra stared blankly at the printed menu in front of her, shaken by her own perfidy, her own shallowness, by what seemed to her a blatant betrayal of the man she had loved. But what dismayed her most of all was the rising tide of physical need, encroaching on her as waves crept inexorably over sand, while she sat there, as helpless as King Canute to order back the sea.

CHAPTER FIVE

ALEXANDRA tried her best to do full justice to the *asperges vinaigrettes*, and the *Cassoulet de Canard* which Dominic told her was his chef's version of a regional speciality. It wasn't that the food was not good. It was excellent. But her awareness of the man sitting opposite her was so acute, so heightened, that it blotted out her response to other stimuli, so she ate without tasting, hoping that he would not realise.

'This is very kind of you. I do hope I haven't wasted too much of your time,' she said formally, as they finished coffee. 'Anyhow, I really should be going now.'

'Got a full appointment book, have you?' he asked a trifle sarcastically, well aware that she knew no one outside the d'Albigny family, and had only his empty apartment awaiting her return. 'It's not a good idea to drive so soon after drinking, Alexandra.'

'I only had two glasses of wine. I should be all right,' she protested. She was anxious now to be away from him, afraid that she might betray something of the emotional turmoil that was racking her. 'Besides, I shouldn't keep you from your work.'

'I should be able to spare an hour for a long-lost relative,' he said flippantly. 'Come on. I'll show you around.'

His hand briefly brushed her arm as he pulled back her chair, and again that almost sickening shock jarred her nerves. Confusion overwhelmed her. She did not understand why, much of the time, he seemed eager to send her as far away as possible—preferably all the way back to England—then, at other times, he appeared reluctant to let her go when she herself would have preferred to.

If he was difficult to read, even less did she understand herself. She had been in love—desperately, unreservedly, or so she had believed—but never once had she felt this gut-churning combination of apprehension and delight she suffered increasingly whenever Dominic touched her. Was it purely and simply sexual attraction? Was it some strange hangover of 'unfinished business' from their youth? Whatever it was, it was growing harder to control, and harder to hide each time they met.

She walked uneasily at his side past the pool, through groves of perfumed shrubs and along quiet pathways, and he showed her the squash and tennis-courts, the gymnasium complex with its whirlpool tubs. Everywhere was deserted. People were either having lunch or enjoying their siesta, and the sun was high and hot in the sky.

'Is the complex finished yet?' Alexandra asked, anxious to break the tense silence which shivered all around them.

'Virtually. I want it to remain small and exclusive. There will be management responsibility, of course, but Chantal will be able to handle most of that, with the assistance of more staff. Ultimately, I'll just retain a watching brief.'

He took a bunch of keys from his pocket. 'Would

you like to see inside one of the villas? This block is finished but not yet sold.'

He turned the key of a ground floor apartment and ushered Alexandra into a cool, tiled hall which led to a pleasantly spacious living-room, already tastefully furnished.

'So what's next—after you are no longer closely involved with this?' she asked. She was aware that her own voice sounded high and quick, and knew that this was because she was so intensely conscious of being alone with him. Really alone, without the safety-net of other people, in a situation where anything could happen. Knowing that although she was scared sick she was nevertheless waiting for it to happen, she moved away quickly, making a pretence of glancing into the gleaming, brand-new kitchen.

'Next?' His voice echoed in the emptiness of the villa. 'Well, it occurred to me that, if one can make a pleasant environment for people to holiday in, it should be equally possible to create something attractive for them to live in all year round. Using the same architect and incorporating some of the ideas we've put into practice, here. I'm negotiating for a plot of land——'

He broke off abruptly. Alexandra had taken a few nervous steps away, avoiding physical closeness, but now she found herself standing in the doorway of one of the cool, shuttered bedrooms, the bed unmade but covered by a fine cotton throw-over. She shivered, her eyes widened, the association of ideas unmistakable.

'You don't really want to know all this, do you?' he asked quietly.

She did not know whether he had brought her here deliberately, or if she had accompanied him for the same purpose. She only knew that the silent message she had sensed winging itself from him to her, in the restaurant, was loud and clear once more, and this time there could be no misunderstanding it. Right now, this minute, he wanted her. She could not be sure he would feel the same way tomorrow, or in an hour's time, but his desire, fusing with her own, was too strong for her to go on fighting. This force was greater than she was, and sooner or later it had to triumph.

It has to be, she thought, as he advanced towards her. I can't escape—I don't want to escape. As if in concert, choreographed to unseen music, they swayed together, she leaned back against the door-jamb, and, his hands resting either side of her face on the white-painted woodwork of the door, he bent his head and possessed her mouth. Like a thirsty traveller at a long-sought oasis, she drank the sweetness of the kiss for which she had waited so long, opening her lips to him, feeling him nip gently but sensually with his teeth before probing with his tongue.

Only their mouths met, neither his hands nor his body had touched hers, and yet fire ran through her. Fire which, crazy as it seemed, left her cold, yearning for the warmth of him against her. When at last he laid the palms of his hands on her breasts, circling them slowly, a strangled cry rose up from within her, so sensitive had she become to his touch. Her arms went around his neck, and now, finally, she was holding him close, her fingers delighting in the thickness of his hair, her body exulting in the hardness of his. He gathered her to him so tightly that she gasped with painful pleasure, his kisses growing fiercer and more demanding, whatever reserve she had left melted in this onslaught of desire.

It needed only a few more such moments to carry them the few feet to the bed. They were very nearly beyond the point of turning back, when the cry of a young child, escaping from the enforced inactivity of an afternoon nap, split the air, and footsteps pattered by on the walkway outside.

'Jamie!' a woman's voice called out sharply in English. 'Come back here, this instant! I didn't say you could go out!'

Alexandra felt the tension snap on inside Dominic, as if he had forcibly pulled a switch, and immediately he released her. She sank back against the wall, still trembling inwardly. His eyes were darker than she had ever seen them, and she could have sworn that he had been as overcome as she by the sudden storm of passion which had swept over them. Why had he brought her here, where he knew they would be alone, if not because he had wanted to make love to her? It must have been obvious to him, from the instant intensity of her response, that she had wanted it just as badly. If that was so, then why had he suddenly stopped, leaving her, leaving them both, suspended on a high point of unsatisfied desire?

For a long moment, neither of them spoke. She longed to ask him why he was behaving so strangely, why he had led her on and then rejected her, but dared not; his face was grim and closed, as if he despised himself for his momentary weakness.

Then he straightened up, and his voice was calm and quite normal as he said, 'I don't suppose anything will now convince you that I don't keep this apartment vacant to seduce potential clients' wives and assorted stray cousins.'

Was he trying to tell her that he had made no more than a routine, casual pass at her, as he might have done had he been alone here with any woman who briefly attracted him? Alexandra could not bear to believe that was all it had been to him, when she had been ready for total surrender to a need too powerful to resist. If she accepted that, it reduced the entire thing to triviality.

'I wasn't on the point of being seduced, Dominic,' she observed gravely. 'It wasn't that one-sided, and you know it.'

'Then maybe you were on the point of seducing me,' he replied with determined facetiousness. He gestured towards the door with his hand, indicating that they should leave, and she preceded him silently, with as much dignity as she could maintain, since he refused to take what had happened seriously.

Only as they emerged into the sunlight, and he locked the door behind them, he said more quietly, 'Don't play that game unless you're willing and able to abide by the rules.'

'*Game?*' she repeated in a low voice, stung, insulted. 'Is that what you call it. . .a game?'

'For me, it is,' he insisted firmly. 'That's all it can be. I don't intend being caught in any emotional traps, or succumbing to the temptation of taking any woman too seriously. For a moment, perhaps, I thought you were like-minded. But you play in a different league, Alexandra. You give all, and more, as you did with Tristan, not knowing when to hold back, when to get the hell out. Like your mo——'

He broke off, tight-lipped. Alexandra stared at him, and in her brain things she had only half understood for years began to slot into place with deadly precision. She did not need him to tell her. She knew. Nevertheless, she said quietly, 'Go on.'

He shook his head. 'Forget it. Let's go.'

'No,' she said stubbornly. 'I can't just forget it. I want this out in the open. You were going to say "like your mother", weren't you? My mother was emotionally involved with someone—someone wrong for her, someone she couldn't have.' Almost there, she picked her way carefully but inexorably. 'Dominic—it was your father, wasn't it?'

'I've said too much already,' he replied curtly. 'I'm sorry, but if you want to know any more, you'll have to ask her.'

Her gaze was blank, incredulous. 'Ask her. . .my mother? But Dominic, that's impossible! She died when I was eighteen!'

The silence between them went on and on, until it seemed interminable. A heavy stone could have dropped without disturbing it. For almost the first time, she saw his guard lowered, a helter-skelter of expressions chasing each other across his face—astonishment, pain, regret, disbelief. Then he said, deathly calm, 'Why didn't you tell me this?'

'I don't know!' she cried wretchedly. 'You never asked, for one thing. It happened a long time ago, and I didn't realise it was important for you to know. *Is* it?'

'Of course it is!' he exclaimed impatiently. 'You kept asking me what had caused the rift, what had happened when we were young. How could I take it on myself to tell you, if one of the people concerned was still alive? If she had wanted you to know, I reckoned she would have told you herself. Obviously, she didn't, but I find it hard to believe that you hadn't put two and two together and worked it out for yourself.'

'Well, I hadn't!' she cried. 'I never suspected, until this moment. When you are young, you never think your parents experience such emotions. You blithely assume that they are past such things! Maybe, if she had lived, she would have told me when I was older, but I'll never know!'

He looked at her as if a vast, impassable gulf separated them, a gulf caused by the knowledge that he had been forced to live with, of which she, until now, had been blessedly ignorant. It seemed impossible that minutes ago they had been in each other's arms.

'Well, you were damned fortunate to have been spared from knowing,' he said harshly. 'I was older than you when it happened, and not so lucky! All her life, she had wanted my father. Marriage between them was not permitted; *he* knew that and accepted that he had to marry someone suitable, for the sake of the estate. Why couldn't she also have accepted that he was not for her?'

Alexandra was swept by a rush of protectiveness for the woman she had never really known. 'Oh, I see. You mean my mother wasn't rich, or titled, or otherwise well connected,' she said scathingly. 'She just loved him. How very remiss of her!'

He glared witheringly at her. 'You must have inherited this bleeding-heart, love-conquers-all notion,' he said coldly. 'Year after year she kept on returning to Château Albigny, even after she was married herself. Lord knows what your father thought—he must have suspected something. Why couldn't she let it go, concentrate on her husband and child, why couldn't she let old feelings die naturally, rather than continually stoking the flames?'

Alexandra was white-faced with anger now. 'Who do you think you are, to condemn my mother in this way?' she demanded fiercely. 'If this affair went on right through our childhood, I might remind you that it takes two to tango! Unless you'd have me believe that your father was bound and gagged first?'

He smiled faintly at this, and Alexandra found his condescension more infuriating than his anger.

'You've got hold of the wrong end of the stick. They were both technically faithful to their marriage vows until that last year, after your father had died. Do you remember that summer?'

The question was rapped out curtly, and Alexandra thought bitterly, As if I could forget! He was the one to whom it had obviously meant very little. But she said only, 'I remember.'

'That's when it happened,' he told her, a wealth of condemnation in his voice. 'Your mother was free, then. There was no longer anything to hold her back.'

Alexandra gave a snort of contempt. 'It's the old "the woman tempted me" syndrome, isn't it? Why is it always *she* who's held responsible? Are you men such innocent, gullible creatures that we deviously clever females can lead you by the nose? It surprises me to hear *you* admit to such a theory!'

Not a flicker of emotion showed on his face now—he confronted her like a stone wall, against which the puny strength of her anger had to quickly exhaust itself.

'You may like it or not, Alexandra, but it's the woman who sets the standards in every society—who draws the lines,' he stated bluntly. 'Men tend to take what they are offered. If there are to be constraints, women have to set them. Your mother failed to do that.'

'Only because she was in love!' Alexandra cried pssionately. 'Maybe it was wrong, but was it such a crime? This was not just a casual affair, but a life-long love. I thought you French understood affairs of the heart.'

'And so we do, if they are conducted discreetly and without hurting others,' he said with icy disdain. 'Is that what you call love? A couple of so-called responsible adult people, one with a son old enough to be at university, rolling about on a bed in the middle of the afternoon without having taken the simple precaution of bolting the door? It was my mother, innocently walking in to show yours a new dress she had bought, who caught them literally in the act. If that's what you call love, then I pass!'

The anger in him was far stronger than mere moral indignation. It encompassed deeper emotions, real distress, pain which was almost tangible. But Alexandra's own feelings were too raw for her to hold out the olive-branch of sympathy.

'What kind of a man are you, Dominic?' she demanded. 'Are you so invulnerable, is your life so blameless, that you can't forgive weakness in others? Have you never felt strongly enough about anyone to understand what such emotions can drive one to do?'

Her outburst appeared not to affect him in the slightest; on the contrary, he regarded her with the utmost cynicism. 'If there's one thing my parents' experience has taught me, it's to avoid such a misfortune at any cost,' he said. 'I've never claimed to be perfect. Yes, I have lovers, from time to time. But I don't mess around with other men's wives. Nor do I promise undying devotion, or anything else I can't deliver. I always say "no strings" and that's precisely what I mean.'

A sudden, acute realisation that this warning was being spelled out directly to her made Alexandra's cheeks flare. Two people rolling about on a bed in the middle of the afternoon—wasn't that precisely where events had been leading them? If there are to be constraints, women have to set them. Would he have liked it better if she had fought him off?

Like mother, like daughter—was that what he was trying to say, lumping them both together in one cold blast of condemnation? Making it clear that he, unlike his father, was not susceptible to 'emotional traps'? She shivered with mortification.

'Don't worry—you aren't, and never have been, in any danger from me!' she declared stoutly. 'I've been in love. When you've known the real thing, you aren't likely to be led astray by the imitation.'

'Bah!' Dominic said dismissively. 'Adolescent sob-stuff! I should have known this would lead us right back to Tristan and this great passion of yours. From where I stand, it seems you simply allowed him to use you, subjugated your own preferences, neglected your work in order to shore up his inadequacies! Just as your mother kept on hankering after a childhood sweetheart, instead of devoting her energies to putting her own house in order. One has to wonder—is this some kind of genetic perversity?'

Alexandra gasped. 'Enough! That's enough! I don't want to hear any more!'

Whirling round, she hurried along the path, breaking into a run as she passed the swimming-pool, but scarcely noticing the puzzled look on Jean-Louis's face as he watched her from the bar. By the time she reached the car park, she was out of breath. Leaning against the car, taking in deep, calming gulps of air, she wondered why she had been running. Because he had made no attempt to follow her.

In spite of all the anger and recriminations they had hurled at one another, she had somehow expected to turn and find him behind her, to feel his hands hard on her shoulders. But he had let her go, without protest, without trying to prevent her, so she had to conclude that he meant every word he had said.

She slid into the driver's seat and started the engine. Even now, she was convinced he could no more have resisted that passionate embrace in the villa than she could herself—that something strong, mutual and irresistible had drawn them into each other's arms.

You've got it wrong again, Alexandra, she told herself sourly. He'd merely been playing a game, a game he admitted he played from time to time, casually and without emotion. Until he remembered that she, like her mother, had an unfortunate tendency to give her heart without reserve, and then he had slammed on the brakes.

Well, he need have no fear. She might have wanted him to make love to her. To be honest, she *had* wanted it, very much. And she might have been in love with him at fifteen. But there was no danger of its happening again. So far as she was concerned, the entire d'Albigny clan could go and run up one of their own vines. She was going home. Tomorrow.

* * *

The doorbell rang at about six-thirty, just as she was fixing herself a cup of coffee and wondering whether she could face anything to eat. Her heart seemed to hang suspended for a moment or two, and she pressed a hand to the space where it should be in an attempt to encourage it to behave normally.

It had to be Dominic. Who else would call here at this time? If the concierge came up to collect any of Dominic's mail it was always during the morning, and she knew no one else.

But why? What did he want? To apologise for the harsh things he had said to her, earlier that afternoon? Alexandra smiled wryly—that did not sound much like Dominic. And, to be fair, she had given as good as she had received in the exchange.

Well, there's only one way to find out, girl, she told herself, and went to open the door, trying not to appear scared and excited at the same time.

He wore jeans and a sweatshirt, looked supremely casual and yet somehow maintained that elegance which never deserted him. 'I've come to take you to a party,' he said airily, strolling in as if he owned the place—which, of course, he did, she reminded herself. He was smiling, unconcerned, as if he had never said such cruel, hurtful words to her only a few hours earlier. It was on the tip of Alexandra's tongue to blurt out her decision to leave, but she checked it. She could not bear to see the certain relief on his face, nor to have him think she was running away from the trauma of further confrontation with him.

'I'm not going anywhere with you, Dominic,' she said coldly. 'You must be crazy to think I'd even consider it.'

'Ah, but this is not just anywhere,' he said confidently, displaying no trace of doubt that he could make her change her mind without any trouble. 'It's the vintage at the château—when we celebrate getting in the grape harvest and give a big party for all the estate workers and staff.'

Despite herself, Alexandra's eyes opened wider. The vintage party was held annually, she knew. She herself had never attended one—they fell in term-time, when she had had to be back at school in England. But she had heard plenty of stories about what great fun they always were, with the entire estate *en fête*. She had always wished that one day she might be in a position to be there at vintage-time, and it was hard to suppress the desire, even now.

'Just say I wanted to go—you've told me many times I'm not welcome at the château,' she said flatly.

'Would I invite you, if that were so?' he asked, and she frowned, puzzled. '*Grand-mère* wants you to come. She greatly regrets the estrangement between the two of you. . .although, of course, she's unlikely to admit it in so many words. She has too much d'Albigny pride.'

'What about *my* pride, or, being a mere commoner, aren't I allowed to have any?' Alexandra demanded angrily. 'I was treated abominably, without being given any explanation, and now you expect me to go crawling back when you crook your little finger? Why should I? And what's changed to make me all of a sudden acceptable, when I was considered a pariah before?'

He shifted his position impatiently, and she sensed his toleration of her protest fading quickly.

'Isn't it obvious? My grandmother's first reaction, on seeing you, was instinctive. You stood there in the hall, without any warning, looking so much like Christine that the past came rushing back to her. And on consideration it seemed likely to us that you were merely the precursor. We thought your mother had sent you on ahead to reconnoitre the ground, to find out if she could come back herself. We did not know she was dead. The split was total and final, and no lines of communication were left open. Until this afternoon, we had no idea.'

'And now it's all right? My mother would never be welcomed back in her lifetime, but I am *persona grata*—just?' she said bitterly. 'How very gracious of you all! How very condescending! I do appreciate the honour you have decided to bestow on me. But the answer is still no—thank you!'

He seemed to uncoil himself to an even greater height, towering over her, the dark eyes no longer amiable but smouldering with impatience.

'Now you listen to me. Personally, I don't give a hoot whether you come or not, but *Grand-mère* is old, she's not well, and at her age there's no way of knowing how long she will last. If she wants you there, she's going to get you. I'm not leaving this apartment unless you leave with me—however long that takes. *Tu comprends?*'

So saying, he flopped easily into a chair, propping his feet on one of the marble-topped tables, and folding his arms across his chest. He had not raised his voice once while making this declaration, but Alexandra did not doubt he would carry out his threat, if necessary, even if it entailed his staying the night.

As their eyes met, he smiled grimly, and she saw that the same thought had occurred to him. 'It could be very boring, unless we find some way of passing the time,' he said softly. 'Perhaps you could suggest something we could do?'

The mere idea of being closeted here with Dominic all through the hours of darkness was enough to send her into a frenzy. Was he threatening to resume the 'game', as he had called it, that he had begun to play with her that afternoon? And if she refused to budge would he draw the conclusion that she was only too eager to continue?

A large part of her was only too well aware that if she felt his mouth, his hands on her once more, she would be unable to resist. The last thing she wanted was for him to sense the full strength of her attraction, but it was not entirely that which made her climb down from her high horse.

It was the thought of Tante Corinne confined to that wheelchair for what remained of a once active life. Tante Corinne, whom she had loved so dearly as a child, who now, for whatever reason, wanted to make amends. Could she vent her rancour on this old lady, however degraded she had felt by the d'Albignys' treatment of her, and the acrimony between Dominic and herself? It was only one evening, and then she would be gone. She need never see any of them again, including this man whose dark eyes glared challengingly at her now, setting her pulse racing even with his anger.

'Very well,' she said stiffly, 'you don't have to threaten me. An evening at the château is a pleasanter prospect than being stuck here with you! I'll come. Do I have to change?'

'Jeans are fine,' he said, accepting his victory without crowing over it. But then, he probably thought it no more than what was due to him. 'My sisters will probably be wearing theirs.'

But mine aren't Fiorucci or Gloria Vanderbilt, Alexandra thought ruefully. What the hell—they would have to accept her as she was. They had always done so in the past.

'Give me five minutes,' she said, and disappeared into the bedroom, closing the door firmly behind her.

She emerged shortly after in clean 501s and a navy and white striped sweatshirt, her face made up, her hair brushed and confined at the nape of her neck with a pale blue chiffon scarf. 'Will I do?' she asked coolly.

The glance he spared her denied that he had any personal interest in how she looked. 'You'll do fine,' he said unconcernedly. 'It's a very casual affair—roast sucking-pig, and plenty of *primeur* to drink. We'll go in my car—it's parked outside.'

It was. A gleaming, metallic-gold Aston Martin, at least twenty years old, in mint condition. Briefly, Alexandra forgot her annoyance with its owner as an admiring cry escaped her. 'Good lord! It's like the one James Bond drove in the 007 movies! It must be practically a collector's item.'

'I like things—and people—that are original, or different,' he stated. 'There aren't too many of this model, from that particular year, in as good shape. I'm not likely to pass another one driving along the street.'

He opened the door to allow her to slide in. 'Watch that wicked tongue of yours. I might just have a lever which operates one of those ejector seats and tosses you out into the night,' he warned, with a faint grin.

Alexandra's wicked tongue very nearly retorted that it might be preferable to what lay ahead. Now that the time had come for her to return to Château Albigny, it appeared ahead of her not as a happily anticipated event, but as an ordeal.

She *was* her mother's daughter after all, and if the family could not quite forget the past, no more could she bury completely her resentment of their attitude—in particular the cold condemnation, the ringing scorn with which Dominic had lashed her that afternoon. She was silent as they left Perpignan behind, the car's headlamps cutting a swathe through the darkened countryside, and deliberately avoided looking at him.

But he picked up her apprehension all the same. 'Worried?' he asked, and amazingly she heard a hint of sympathy in his voice.

'Wouldn't you be, in my place?' she asked warily. 'I feel as if I have inherited so much anger, so much pain. . .like an unwanted legacy. And for what? One brief lapse of conduct, a long time ago.'

She sensed his shake of the head. 'You miss the point. It wasn't just that. It was all that followed from it, for us as a family,' he said quietly. 'You see. . .although there was no question of a divorce, my parents were left shackled together in a relationship which was going nowhere. My mother loved my father very deeply. . .she suffered very much. And, I have to say, he did nothing to make amends for her suffering. The atmosphere was unbearable, and it affected us all. *Grand-mère* fell ill, and never really recovered. It seemed we would never be happy again.'

There was no recrimination in the calm, matter-of-fact voice in the car's dark interior. He was simply stating what he knew to be true, and Alexandra had to accept it, as she had been unable to do earlier in the day when they had shouted at one another in anger.

'I had no idea. I'm sorry,' she said. 'I never thought of it that way. . .never realised a love-affair could have so many dreadful repercussions.'

'Well. . .' His hands moved lightly on the wheel as he turned the car on to the private road. 'I think the younger ones escaped the worst. Sabine and Danielle now have happy marriages. Michel fancies himself as a playboy, but hopefully he'll slow down and start behaving responsibly before too long. None of it was your fault. Your only crime was to turn up unannounced, looking like your mother.'

Alexandra wondered wretchedly whether they were all looking at her through the wrong end of a telescope. All right, her hair was the same colour, she was roughly the same height, but there it ended. Unfortunately. If she had had half her mother's beauty and charm, she would not have let the boy she had loved slip through her fingers. Instead, he would have been her first lover, and the whole course of her life might have run differently. The lonely years believing herself unattractive, the despair, the chaos of her affair with Tristan. . .she might have been spared so much anguish. How simple, how good it could have been, if Dominic had only loved her in the beginning!

The longing implicit in this thought startled her so much that she fell silent again, and was glad he did not press her to say anything more. And then at last they arrived at Château Albigny, and it would have been a dour spirit which did not lift at the scene before them.

The trees around the house were festooned with brightly coloured small lights, red, blue, yellow, and on the open space beyond the formal lawns spits were turning, filling the air with the aroma of succulently roasting meat. Trestle tables groaned under the weight of bowls of salad, fruit, pâté, platters of cheese and long, crusty baguettes of bread, and there were huge barrels of the young wine, which was being liberally dispensed.

People were milling everywhere, laughing, talking, with the happy release of a successfully concluded year's work—a good vintage, safely in. Someone was playing an accordian, and there were sporadic bursts of cheerful singing.

Dominic took Alexandra's arm as they got out of the car, and led her through the throng. Men ran up and pumped his hand, he slapped them on the back, laughing, and kissed the girls on both cheeks uninhibitedly. Alexandra found herself grabbed and kissed too, by complete strangers, a huge goblet brimful of wine thrust into her hand. She could not help but be seized by the zest and joyfulness of it all, and her grey-green eyes sparkled with excitement as she looked up at Dominic.

'How marvellous! Everything I used to hear about vintage is true! Everyone is so happy—it's as if they were each personally responsible for it!' she enthused.

'As they are, in a way,' he agreed. 'It's very much a team effort, working a vineyard. Many of these people's families have worked on the estate for generations. It belongs to them as surely as it belongs to us. We give them their livelihoods, they give us their labour. Symbiosis—we couldn't survive without each other.'

Out here in the crowded night, where she was virtually anonymous, Alexandra felt at ease. But when he said, 'Come and meet *Grand-mère*. She'll be waiting for you,' she swallowed nervously, suddenly afraid once more.

'She'll be very hurt if you don't,' he said, sensing her reluctance. 'Yes, I know she hurt you, but why compound it?'

Why, indeed? Alexandra thought soberly. Suddenly, she was glad she had come tonight, glad to have seen the château again, even if it was for the last time. She would make her peace with Tante Corinne, lay the uneasy ghost of her mother to rest, and then. . .then, as Dominic had advised her, take up the threads of her own life again, as she knew she must.

The old lady was sitting in her wheelchair on the terrace, a warm shawl wrapped around her thin shoulders. She watched them approach, the tall, lithe figure of her grandson holding the arm of the slender, red-headed girl with anxious eyes and bravely set shoulders.

'*Grand-mère*,' he said simply, 'here's Alexandra.'

Tante Corinne's smile was reserved—after all, as Dominic had reminded Alexandra, she was conscious of her dignity—but there was both warmth and regret behind it, and Alexandra realised with some surprise that the old Comtesse was as nervous as she.

'Welcome home, child,' she said. 'How tall you've grown—and how lovely.'

Me? Lovely? Alexandra thought ruefully, but that kindness melted her inhibitions, and she took the thin, claw-like hand that was held out to her. 'I'm happy to be here, Tante Corinne,' she said.

They talked for a few minutes, mostly about Alexandra's studies. Dominic stayed with them, and, when he thought that this first, ice-breaking encounter had lasted long enough, he gently steered Alexandra away. 'You see?' was all he said.

And then a slim, vivacious young woman came flying down the terrace steps towards them, dark curls bobbing, eyes alight.

'Lexi! Lexi! It's you—it really is!' she cried, flinging both arms around Alexandra, who knew her at once and would have known her if she had met her anywhere on the street.

'Dani! I don't believe it! Look at you!' she exclaimed, and hugged her in return, tears springing to her eyes. Little Danielle, a year her junior and her best friend from those far-off days, all grown up but somehow unchanged.

'This is no place for a mere male. I think I can safely leave you girls to your own devices,' Dominic said with a laconic grin.

'*Tiens*, yes, go away—we don't need you!' his sister grinned, linking her arm through Alexandra's and leading her away. 'Now—tell me everything. Dominic refused to say a word about you. Are you married? Any children? What do you do?'

So far as Danielle was concerned, there was no constraint at all. It was as though she had simply been waiting for the signal to welcome Alexandra back to the fold. Together, still chatting, they helped themselves to food and more wine. Danielle introduced Alexandra to her husband, Guy, and took her indoors to the nursery for a peep at her sleeping baby daughter.

Sabine was more reserved in her greeting, but her smile was sincere enough. Both the girls' husbands were involved in the running of the estate in one capacity or another, both were pleasant, personable young men, and, as Dominic had said, his sisters were happily married.

His brother Michel was not quite so easy to define. On the surface he appeared ebullient and cheerful, putting himself about, squeezing and kissing any girl he made contact with, giving everything female the eye. The kiss he gave Alexandra was more than cousinly, and she freed herself quietly but firmly from his over-enthusiastic embrace, wondering if Dominic was watching. She sensed a wildness in Michel. Where their parents' unhappy marriage had left Dominic cynical and wary, his brother's reaction was a capacity for unruliness and disorder.

'He drinks and chases women too much,' Dominic commented, appearing at her side and following her gaze with his own. 'It's the devil's own job to pin him down to steady work. I don't know what the answer is, for him.'

'The right woman, perhaps, when she happens along,' Alexandra suggested.

'Of course, that's your answer to everything, isn't it?' he said, with mild scorn. 'Ever the incurable romantic. Unfortunately, I don't buy that theory.'

She looked at him sharply, and inside her something snapped. 'Perhaps you should at least give it some credence,' she retorted. 'Just because your parents' marriage was disastrous, that doesn't mean it can't work for anyone else. It doesn't mean you should never allow yourself to love.'

He laughed harshly. 'I don't recall asking for your advice, but, if you like, I'll tell you what it means,' he said. 'It means that I'll never risk hurting any woman as my father hurt my mother, and I'll certainly never allow *any* woman to do that to me.'

'Dominic, that's crazy,' she said incredulously. 'Are you going to condemn yourself to a solitary existence, without a wife and children? Don't you think that's taking self-preservation too far?'

'Don't be naïve, Alexandra,' he said contemptuously. 'I never said I intended to remain single. For one thing, I have a duty to this place. If I don't provide it with heirs, Michel is next in line, and on his present showing I don't feel too sanguine about that possibility.'

Alexandra was aware of a sick sensation which had nothing to do with the wine she had just drunk. 'So you'll marry without love?' she asked. 'Don't you think you'll have a little difficulty filling that position?'

'You think so?' he said, with a knowing smile.

He laid a hand on her shoulder, turning her slightly and indicating with a slight gesture of his head a couple who had just arrived and were getting out of their car. The man was tall, spare, balding, in his fifties and with a pompous manner. The girl accompanying him was one of the prettiest Alexandra had ever seen. Young— not more than eighteen or nineteen—with a perfect little oval face framed by a cloud of spun-gold hair. No jeans for her, her slim, beautiful body was enhanced by a subtly draped dress of silky azure which clung to her firm young breasts and taut stomach.

'Who are they?' Alexandra asked curiously.

'The Paulins—father and daughter,' he replied. 'Near neighbours of ours. They own a country house a few miles away. There's the answer to your question, Alexandra: Nathalie Paulin. She's the girl I shall most probably marry.'

CHAPTER SIX

IN THE minutes that followed this declaration, Alexandra congratulated herself sourly on behaving with perfect normality, betraying no excessive emotion at all, smiling, talking, laughing, just as everyone else was doing. After all, what difference did it make to her whom Dominic married, or if he went into it as a cold-blooded, loveless arrangement?

'How nice,' she replied frivolously. 'Does she know?'

He smiled. 'No proposals have been made or accepted, if that's what you mean,' he said. 'But she won't be averse.'

'My—for conceit, you take the gold medal!' she declared with a short laugh, and he looked down at her with an odd gleam in his eyes.

'To becoming Comtesse d'Albigny, I meant. I wasn't referring to my personal charms,' he informed her. 'Paulin *père* is a wine wholesaler—he would be pleased to make his marketing facilities available to the château, in return for marrying his daughter to a title; and the château, for all its becoming a viable concern again, could use those outlets.'

'It all sounds positively nineteenth century to me—rather like something out of Dickens, or Mrs Gaskell,' Alexandra said lightly, trying to sound as if the idea amused her. But there was a weird sensation inside her, as of a large stone settling, or a heavy door closing—a sense of finality, of unattainable dreams, and all the buoyant gaiety that had possessed her earlier had drained away.

'Maybe it does, to you, but it's the way things are done in families like ours, and there's more at stake here than airy-fairy notions of romance,' he said curtly. 'What's so wrong with my marrying Nathalie, anyway? You can't deny that she's a pretty girl. She's been well educated, up to a point, but not so highly that she will have ideas beyond herself. She'd make a very biddable wife, and, of course, she would have everything she wanted, including a château and a perfect husband.'

His expression did not alter, and Alexandra looked directly into his eyes, trying to detect the source of the flicker of irony she discerned in his voice.

'You mean, she wouldn't give you too much trouble?' she heard her own voice say cattily. 'That should make for a pleasantly boring marriage, shouldn't it? And would you manage to remain faithful to her, and not stray off the rails, even though you were not in love?'

'Need you ask?' He virtually attacked her with the question, his eyes cold and hard. 'That's one thing *my* wife won't have to worry about. I may have no time for nebulous concepts such as love, but I won't cause her embarrassment by hankering after some other female I can't have.'

Alexandra stood rock-still as the Paulins walked across the lawn towards them. She smiled and murmured appropriate greetings as she was introduced as 'my cousin from England'. Monsieur Paulin showed off his knowledge of her country by boasting about the number of English cities where he had business contacts. Nathalie merely smiled sweetly and demurely, mostly at Dominic, gazing at him with huge, violet eyes. Maybe nothing had been said expressly, but the girl knew well enough that she was under consideration, Alexandra thought, and she was behaving impeccably, putting not a toe out of line. It was difficult to imagine her throwing a tantrum, or shouting abuse...or being willing to give herself wantonly to a man in the bedroom of a holiday villa...

Alexandra smiled until her face ached, and made inconsequential small talk, the subjects of which she could not remember afterwards. As soon as it was humanly possible, she made an excuse and slipped away, dodging into the laughing crowd and looking for somewhere quiet to escape to.

By instinct, her feet found a remembered path which led around the back of the house to where the stables were. Here there was no one about, and the sounds of revelry reached her only indistinctly, allowing her mind to blot them out.

I don't *care*, she told herself insistently. Why should I? Look at it logically. I had this stupid infatuation with Dominic as a girl, which came to nothing, then I came back, and there's some sort of sexual chemistry which attracts me to him. That's all.

Then why did she feel so sad, not just for herself, but for him, for the uninspired, loveless life to which he was sentencing himself? For the potential to love, which she was sure was in him, which had always been in him, which he was determined to stifle forever?

Alexandra slipped quietly into the stable, smelling the familiar scents of tack and horseflesh, hearing the soft whickers of the animals in their stalls, nervously aware of her presence. She spoke softly to them to allay their fear of her strangeness, and as she approached a soft whinny answered her, as though. . .as though her voice and her smell were recognised. Her eyes becoming accustomed to the gloom, she smiled and drew closer to the noble, black-maned head gazing at her over the stall.

'Dauphin, old boy,' she said gently. 'You're still here? Not so young as you once were, are you?'

Without fear, for this was an old friend, she reached out and stroked the velvety nose, and the black horse blew softly down his nostrils, accepting her presence. She leaned her head against him and gave in to the wave of sadness she could no longer fight.

Dominic. Dominic, who had ridden this horse at her side so long ago. Dominic, who had turned her out of the château but taken her into his home, who had dragged her, mentally and bodily, from the chaotic wreckage of her life and forced her, unwilling, on the path to recovery. Fought with her, castigated her, but kept—she saw, now—a guiding eye on her nevertheless. Made her think. Made her feel. Caused her to start living again.

Dominic, married to that seductively lovely, violet-eyed girl in the blue dress, who would for the rest of her life ride with him, ski with him, sit with him at the long table in the château's dining-room. Have his children, sleep in his bed, make love with him, and preside over all the vintages to come.

I can't come back here, she thought. Never again, after tonight. This place and this man can no longer be part of my life. They belong to *her*.

'Alexandra?'

She started a little as she heard his voice, but did not turn, because she could not bear to look at him.

'I thought I might find you here,' he said. 'You always loved the horses.'

And I always came here if anything upset or troubled me, she thought. He must not know what had sent her running for refuge here tonight.

'I. . . I had a bit of a headache and needed somewhere quiet,' she lied. 'I'm glad to see that Dauphin is still here.'

'Oh, yes. More staid now, in his old age, but I would not want to part with him.'

They looked at one another through the shadowy gloom. He looked calm and composed, and, indeed, why shouldn't he? He had it all worked out, and there was no room in his life for the emotions which played havoc with hers. He had made that very plain to her tonight.

Silently, she said goodbye to him, etching on her mind all the details of the face she thought she would not see again after today. He had become too important to her, but she had only herself to blame for that. He had been right in the beginning—there was really no place for her here. She had found her family again, and now she must lose them, for in running here to escape from pain she had only found more.

'Dominic, I think I should like to go home now,' she said. 'Could you phone me a taxi?'

'There's no need for that. I brought you, so if you want to go I'll drive you back myself,' he said shortly. 'Anyhow, I've no intention of revelling too late. I have to be at Roussillon Village early tomorrow, so I shan't be joining the many who will have sore heads in the morning. Do you want to say goodbye to the family before you go?'

'No—please. Make my excuses for me when you get back,' she said quickly. That was more than she could have endured, knowing that she would not be here again. 'It was lovely to see them all, and I'm grateful for the invitation.' She frowned, and an expression of regret clouded her face. 'Although there's one person I haven't seen. Tante Françoise—your mother.'

She caught the brief hesitation before he said, 'You could not have seen her, because she isn't here. My mother doesn't live at Château Albigny any more. She moved out shortly after my father died, and took a house in a small village up in the hills. She tends to keep to herself most of the time, and doesn't enjoy large gatherings. She paints a lot and quite enjoys her solitary existence.'

'I see. But I would have thought she would have been here tonight, for the vintage.' She paused, and his lack of response told her what she needed to know. 'It's because of me she stayed away, isn't it? She doesn't want to meet me.'

He did not deny it. 'Don't take it too much to heart,' he advised. 'She just isn't ready yet.'

So she was still not fully accepted, Alexandra thought as they left the stables together. It had been an illusion to believe that she could be. Perhaps it was as well that she was leaving.

People were beginning to dance as they walked to where he had left the car, and she thought it must be an irksome duty for Dominic to have to drive her back to Perpignan. He would doubtless be glad to get back to the party and dance with Nathalie. She imagined the golden head resting on his shoulder, fair and dark, close together.

Maybe if the girl played her cards very cleverly, and did not crowd him with too much overt emotion, too many demands for commitment, he might one day grow to love her, despite himself. She understood that it could happen, in marriages which started out as purely business arrangements. Or maybe Nathalie did not care, and would be content simply to call herself Comtesse d'Albigny. Alexandra could not decide which outcome would please her the least.

They did not talk much during the drive, and he seemed preoccupied, although she had no way of knowing what was on his mind. When he parked outside the apartment, he did not suggest coming up with her. He seemed anxious to be off—a man who had discharged his duty by taking her back to the château and at least partially healing the breach. His responsibility for her ended here, and she thought he was most probably glad of it. He would shed no tears over her departure, when he learned of it.

'Goodnight, Alexandra. Sleep well,' he said.

'Goodnight, Dominic. Thank you for a lovely evening.'

'*De rien.*' He watched her enter the lobby before starting the engine, and she hurried to the lift without looking back.

'Goodbye, my love,' she murmured inanely, and then gave herself a mental shake. What was she thinking of?

In the morning, she knew she could not do it—not like this. She had packed her case, phoned to check train and flight times and availability of seats, and was ready to leave when it struck her that if she walked away without telling him she was going, without thanking him for his help and the use of his apartment, then her coming here had all been for nothing. She would still be running, still refusing to face herself. It was easier, yes, but it was the coward's way out.

Alexandra looked at her watch. He had said he would be at Roussillon Village this morning. She had time to drive out there, see him—briefly—then come back and return the hired car before catching the train to Montpellier.

She put her case in the car, gave the key to Madame la Concierge, who expressed surprise and tried unsuccessfully to hide her curiosity, and then she took the road to Canet. And inside her, in spite of everything, there was a fugitive gladness because she would see Dominic once again.

The sun was shining on the white- and pink-washed walls of Roussillon Village, and although October was now well advanced the day was pleasantly warm. In the reception, instead of the super-efficient Chantal, Alexandra found a very harassed Jean-Louis, hopping back and forth like a demented Yo-Yo. Behind him in the office were several telephones, all of which seemed to be ringing at once, and it was some time before he could spare a minute to attend to her.

'Please forgive me,' he said distractedly. 'I am like a crazy man this morning. Chantal has sprained her ankle and will be unable to come in for several days. Usually, there are two assistants, but one is away on a training course, and the other has been so inconsiderate as to catch the flu. Soon I shall have to attend to the restaurant, and then there is the bar...'

'Oh, dear,' Alexandra said sympathetically. 'You really are in the soup. But Dominic won't leave you to cope alone, surely? Where is he?'

Jean-Louis gave a grimace of despair. 'At the château. There are problems there, too, apparently, and I don't know when he wil be able to get away. Madame the old Comtesse has been taken ill, and he can't leave her.'

'But I saw her last night, and she was fine,' Alexandra cried, concerned.

Then she recalled Dominic saying, 'Grand-mère is old...there's no way of knowing how long she will last,' and she knew that the old lady's health was far from good.

She and Jean-Louis looked at one another anxiously. Then one of the telephones began to ring again, and he said, 'Excuse me...' and hurried away. After a few minutes, he returned. 'Mademoiselle Warner, I am so sorry about this. How can I help you?'

Alexandra smiled and shrugged. 'It would appear to be the other way round, *mon ami*,' she said. 'How can I help *you*?'

He looked startled as she lifted the hatch and came round the desk. 'Go and see to the bar and restaurant. I'll stay here and hold the fort for you.'

'Oh, *mademoiselle*, I couldn't...' he said, flustered. 'It is unfair to ask it of you. Besides, you——'

'Besides, I know nothing about this business. You are quite right,' she agreed soberly. 'But I can answer telephones and take messages, at least until things are quieter and you can take over.' She grinned. 'Oh, and by the way, my name is not "*mademoiselle*". It's Alexandra.'

He looked at her, undecided, not sure if he should sanction her access to the inner sanctum of the office even if she was Dominic's cousin. But pressure of work won out over his reluctance; he appeared to decide he could trust her, if a little uncertainly, and hurried away, promising that he would be back as soon as possible.

'Don't worry, I'll find you if I need you—if there is anything I can't handle, or that can't wait,' she said. And then she was alone in her new, if very temporary domain.

So much for my quick getaway, she thought ruefully. But it was no good. She could not leave until she knew that Tante Corinne was going to be all right, and maybe Dominic would not thank her for interfering, but neither could she walk out of Roussillon Village knowing how badly help was needed. Although precisely what she would have to do, she wasn't at all sure.

In the office, the telephone shrilled imperiously. Alexandra picked up the receiver. 'Roussillon Village,' she said, with a confidence she was far from feeling.

And then the morning flew. There were calls about bookings, calls from contractors about development plans, private business calls for Dominic. Residents came by Reception wanting information, reporting small repairs and attention required to their properties. Alexandra dealt with what she could, and noted what she could not, to be attended to later.

She opened and sorted mail as best she was able, took messages which came over the chattering fax machine—fortunately, they had one in her college faculty, so it was no mystery to her. If all else failed, she smiled politely, looked friendly, and above all was *there*. It was just as well she scarcely had time to worry about what was happening at Château Albigny.

It was almost lunchtime when she lifted her head from answering the internal telephone which stood on the reception counter and looked directly into Dominic's enquiring dark eyes. He looked strained and tired, but his white shirt was as crisp as ever, his hair brushed, his demeanour alert. He didn't speak, but she replied to the question his raised dark eyebrows posed.

'I stopped by, and it seemed you needed another pair of hands,' she said. 'How is Tante Corinne?'

He ran a hand through his hair, briefly revealing the scar on his temple that looked white by comparison with his tanned skin—as it always did if he was angry or worried, she thought, with a leap of compassion.

'She's resting. The doctor came and prescribed some different medication, but I'm afraid the trouble is just part of her condition,' he said. 'It will take a few days before we will know if she'll be as good as before, or——' he paused, frowned '—or be permanently bedridden. If the latter, then I'm afraid it will finish her. She loathes inactivity as it is.'

Without thinking, Alexandra laid her hand over his. Sympathy prompted her, but oh, she loved the touch of him, the feel of his skin. She wanted to put her arms round him and hold him, and tell him it would be all right, she would do whatever she could—but she dared not do that, nor would he want her to. It was as well the counter was between them.

'She's strong-willed and determined,' she reassured him. 'She won't just give up, I'm sure.'

He forced an abstracted smile. 'You're right. And thank you for helping out.'

'You're welcome. Actually, I'm thinking of jacking in my PhD and making some man an efficient secretary, instead.' How difficult it was, now, to talk seriously to him without betraying her growing involvement. She was obliged to take refuge in silly jokes.

He flipped through the messages she had taken. 'You haven't done too badly, it would appear,' he said, with surprised approval. 'However, I have a site meeting about the land I'm buying in half an hour, then I must call by the château. These will just have to wait until later. But you must feel free to go—it's not your problem.'

She sighed exasperatedly. 'Of course it's my problem, if it's your problem,' she declared forcibly. 'Am I part of this family, or am I not?'

'That's not at issue,' he said quickly.

'Isn't it?' She planted both hands squarely on the counter, suppressing the urge to smooth the lines from his forehead with her palms. 'Look—you're going to be preoccupied for a few days, and Chantal won't be here to run things for you. I'm willing to help. I'd *like* to help, although I'm aware I won't be capable of doing half of what she normally does. But I owe you one for the loan of your apartment, and. . .and other things. Let me repay it.'

'You owe me nothing,' he insisted, the frown deepening. 'But—as friends, as cousins—all right, I accept your offer.'

There was a brief, curious silence, alive with strange undercurrents, as they locked gazes. Alexandra could feel him reaching out to her, trying to tell her, or ask her something vital. But this wasn't the time, and almost immediately he straightened up, becoming brisk and practical.

'Right. First of all, you can phone some of these people back, if I give you the appropriate answers. And then. . .can you use a computer?'

'There are such things in modern university faculties,' she assured him, po-faced, and he essayed a sketchy grin.

'Then you might like to get to grips with itemising and breaking down these accounts. Previous records will give you an idea of how it's done. If a Mr Vogel calls from New York—it will be later on, because of the time difference—tell him I'll call him back today, without fail. Oh, and ring Philippe Plessis—you'll find his number in my personal address book—and cancel our squash game for this week. Got all that?'

She smiled. 'Aye aye, Cap'n.'

A faint, jaunty cheerfulness brightened the worried face. 'You might not be so light-hearted by the end of the day! Get Jean-Louis to relieve you while you take lunch in the restaurant. Don't pay for anything, just sign a chit.' He glanced swiftly at his thin gold Rolex. 'Time and site engineers wait for no man. *Au revoir.*'

Alexandra was kept fully occupied throughout the day, and, miraculously, she coped. Her French, which had grown increasingly fluent with every day she spent here, stood up well to the onslaught, although talking on the telephone presented more problems than addressing someone face to face. If the office did not run with the well-oiled precision of Chantal's management, at least it was manned, and there were no great disasters, she thought wryly.

She ignored Dominic's instructions to have lunch in the restaurant. Jean-Louis was himself too busy to relieve her, so she had him send her a coffee and a sandwich, which she ate as she tussled with the accounts.

Reception closed officially at six-thirty, and, although she was tired and had the beginnings of a headache, Alexandra was aware of a glow of satisfaction. The work she had done today was completely different from the academic endeavours which occupied her working day back in Oxford, but she had survived. She had even enjoyed herself, in a way.

Dominic came back just as she was closing the office. Glancing at the empty cup and plate on her desk, he said accusingly, 'I see you took no notice of what I said about lunch. There are penalties for disobeying the boss, you know.'

'I'm terrified,' she said, then, looking beyond the deliberately cheerful grin to the tired, troubled eyes and creased forehead, she added quietly, 'How are things at the château?'

'The same. There's no change, as yet.' He sighed. 'Come on—let's go grab a quick meal, then I must take over the bar and let Jean-Louis sign off. He's been hard at work all day.'

As have you, in one way or another, she wanted to point out, but knew it would have little effect. As the owner, he would fully accept the necessity to run himself into the ground to keep things going smoothly. She did not refuse his offer of a meal. If he had company while he ate he might sit down a few minutes longer, she reasoned, and he looked as if he needed the break.

However, he ordered nothing more time-consuming than omelettes and salad and a small carafe of wine, followed by black coffee, and she knew there would be no lingering over the table. They were eating not for pleasure but simply because they had to, in order to keep going.

As they finished the coffee, he said, 'It occurred to me that if you are going to be here for a few days it would be easier if you slept in one of the villas. So I called by the apartment, thinking you would not object if I took the liberty of packing a few essentials for you.'

Alexandra jumped. Her hurried departure this morning and the reason why she had come to Roussillon Village in the first place had been all but forgotten, swallowed up in the urgency of the day. He noted her half-guilty expression.

'Yes,' he said, 'it came as rather a surprise to me when the concierge told me you had left.'

The faint note of accusation in his voice took Alexandra by surprise. She had thought he would be only too relieved to see the back of her. 'I came to tell you I was going back to England,' she said defensively.

He regarded her steadily, and she felt his eyes penetrating the recesses of her soul, seeking out the reasons for her action.

'It must have been a sudden decision. You said nothing about leaving the night before, at the party.'

'Yes and no,' she hedged, struggling like a butterfly pinned on a board, trying not to betray that it was what he himself had said to her about his marriage plans which had swayed her decision. 'I'd thought about it, on and off. I do have work to go back to, as you keep reminding me, and it seemed to me I had accomplished as much as I could hope for, *vis-à-vis* the family. There was no point in hanging on. You all have your lives to lead, your futures planned. . .as do I.'

She kept her voice and her expression deliberately calm and unemotional as she said this. His *mariage de convenance* was nothing to do with her, and she had no right to the painful feelings the thought of it aroused. Above all, she must ensure that he remained unaware of them.

He returned her gaze thoughtfully, before saying quietly, 'It seems to me your mind was well made up. But you are still here. So, what now?'

She forced a shrug. I'm here because I care too much. . .about the family. . .and about you in particular, was not an answer she dared give him, for all it was the truth.

'A few more days won't harm. I. . . I couldn't leave without knowing Tante Corinne was going to be all right, so I might just as well make myself useful while I'm here.'

'Of course. You were always fond of her,' he said flatly. 'Well, you certainly have been useful today, and I'm appreciative.'

'There's no need for gratitude. We're quits,' she told him. After a brief hesitation, she went on, 'I'm glad we met again, Dominic, and I hope the future works out well for you—with the vineyard, and your other business interests. And with Nathalie, if that's what you want.'

The worst irony was that she really meant it. She really did want him to find happiness, even though she would be no part of it.

'What I want?' he echoed gravely. 'We do what we

must, Lexi. I'll marry and provide heirs for the château. You'll sail through your degree and become a world-renowned expert on romantic poetry.' His dark eyes held hers, briefly. 'Be sure to find a real man, next time. You deserve better.'

Alexandra was biting back tears as she fetched her suitcase from the car, and she followed him to the villa he had allocated for her. His sudden, unexpected use of her childhood nickname, his final piece of advice were too poignant. It was like a farewell. Oh, she might be here for a few days yet, but their relationship was wound up. It had gone as far as it could go. He was content with that, maybe, but she knew that she was not.

She worked for two more days at Roussillon Village, giving everything she had, partly because there was plenty to do, most of it new and demanding for her, but partly because keeping frenziedly busy blotted out the possibility of too much thinking.

Dominic called by from time to time, to take his messages and deal with matters only he could attend to, and reported, grim-faced, that Tante Corinne's condition showed little improvement.

'I'm terribly afraid that we're going to lose her,' was all he said, and Alexandra could offer little by way of comfort, for all she longed to.

At night she flopped exhausted into bed in the villa, and hoped sleep would overcome her quickly, before the thought of Dominic began to haunt her. The strength of her obsession with him troubled her deeply. Anyone would think she was in love with him, but she *couldn't* be. It wasn't possible. She had come to France still struggling to come to terms with the loss of one man. How could she fall so quickly for another? It's nothing but sex, she told herself dismissively. Physical attraction, which would fade when she removed herself from its sphere of influence.

'Chantal phoned to say she will be back tomorrow,' Jean-Louis told her on the third-morning, setting a cup of coffee on the reception counter for Alexandra. 'She says she can hobble about, and is anxious to get back to work. Martine is recovering from the flu, and won't be absent much longer. And next week Sylvie returns from her course, so we shall be at full strength once more.'

'That's good.' Alexandra smiled, wishing she did not feel so bereft. Her usefulness was quickly coming to an end. 'You won't be needing me, then.'

'Ah, but you have been invaluable. *Formidable*,' he said quickly, gallantly. 'Without you, I don't know what we would have done here at the village.' He smiled back. 'There is an English saying, Dominic told me last night—"blood is thicker than water". No?'

So that's why I'm here, she thought ruefully. Or, at least, that's why he thinks I'm here. Tonight she must make it clear to Dominic that she understood he did not really need her any more. It would be too embarrassing to wait until he pointed it out to her. And Tante Corinne? She was holding her own, and it might be that she would remain indefinitely as she was now. If she was not in immediate danger, Alexandra knew it would be wrong and foolish of her to use the old lady as an excuse to overstay her welcome. She should go—and soon.

But Dominic did not turn up that evening. Alexandra closed the office, ate a solitary dinner in the restaurant, and still there was no sign of him, nor even a telephone call. She was still worrying about what might be happening at the château as she walked back along the quiet, flower-scented pathway to her villa and let herself in.

There's nothing you can do, she told herself wearily, as she kicked off her shoes and made herself coffee. If there was a crisis they would not welcome her phoning up and distracting them with enquiries, and it could simply be that Dominic was too busy, too tired, or was unable to get away for any number of reasons.

Alexandra loosened her hair, shook it free, and sank into an armchair, stretching out thankfully. She closed her eyes and went through the process of deliberately shutting out thoughts that weren't good for her. Tomorrow, she really would leave. They no longer needed her here, and it was time to draw a line under this strange, bittersweet chapter of her life.

Sighing deeply, she let her head fall back, and drifted into a restless sleep.

CHAPTER SEVEN

ALEXANDRA dreamed that someone's hand was gently stroking her cheek, a touch that was soft and caressing, and yet, at the same time, generated stirrings of excitement. And then she opened her eyes to find that she was not dreaming, and that the hand now brushing her forehead was Dominic's. He was kneeling at her side, looking into her face with an expression of tender concern, tinged by something deeper, stranger—a yearning need.

She moved slowly, resting her head against his palm, still in that odd state between sleeping and waking, shot through by a filmic unreality.

'Mm. . . Dominic. . .how did you get in? I didn't hear you.'

'I used my pass key. And I'm not surprised you didn't. You look exhausted, *pauvre petite*.'

She gazed sleepily into his eyes and saw that they too were glazed with tiredness; his hair was dishevelled, his shirt, for once, crumpled as if he'd had no time to change. 'So do you,' she murmured.

A smile lifted the lines of his face, and she realised that the worried preoccupation which had shrouded him for the last few days had eased. He was simply tired, no longer a man walking under a shadow.

'Tante Corinne?' she asked quickly, hopefully.

'Much better. More like her old self. The treatment

appears to be working, and the doctor thinks she may be able to get up for a short while tomorrow.'

'Oh, Dominic—I'm so glad!'

Spontaneously her arms went around his neck, without her having planned that they should, drawing his head against her breasts, and for a brief while he rested there accepting the warmth and comfort of her body, the pair of them like sleepwalkers, scarcely aware of what they did. And then, as she felt the touch of his mouth just above her heart, exhaustion left her like a ghost fleeing daylight. A tingling glow began to spread from the point where his lips moved lightly, disturbing the thin lawn of her dress and making her skin burn beneath it.

Slowly, he raised his head; as in a dream, hers bent to meet it, and their lips joined. A flash-fire enveloped her at the contact, and from that moment she stopped fighting, stopped caring what might happen afterwards. She accepted that this must be, that she wanted him now, no matter what.

Without a word he lifted her from the chair, carried her through to the half-darkened bedroom and the waiting bed. She moaned with impatience as he unfastened her clothes and removed them, her fingers shamelessly undoing the buttons of his shirt and running over the finely haired muscles of his chest.

'*Mon dieu*, you're beautiful,' he said hoarsely.

Yesterday she would have ruefully denied it, but now, with his hands eagerly and skilfully discovering her, she believed.

'So are you,' she said wonderingly. And, truly, he was. She had never known a man's body could arouse such desire and admiration, never known there could be not merely pleasure, but such urgent, driving need. Alexandra could hardly bear this anticipation, every inch of her skin shivering with response to his touch; she could hardly wait for the moment when she felt him inside her, and knew she was his.

And now the glow was in the very core of her being, radiating out from the quivering centre, the feeling too intense to be endured. She was out of control, on a rocket heading for the limits of the universe, leaving the stars behind. She cried out—a low, female cry of triumph and surrender, and then she was floating somewhere, serene and at peace, knowing that there was nothing more she could possibly need.

It was a small death, a moment of oblivion, and she came to to find herself lying wrapped in his arms. He smiled and drew her head against his shoulder, and with a deep, fulfilled sigh she let sleep claim her.

She awoke to find the sounds of morning—birdsong, distant voices—and importunate sunlight invading through the half-closed shutters. Blinking against the sudden brightness, she found herself alone among the disorder of the bedclothes; the quilt had slipped down below her waist, her hair was tousled over her forehead and in her eyes.

She stretched luxuriantly, savouring blissfully for a few moments the delicious memories of the night, waiting for him to come back to her. Perhaps he was in the shower, or making coffee. She smiled. Coffee would be lovely, sitting up in bed together. And then. . .she could hardly wait for it to happen again. . .

Then the very silence of the place hit her. There were no footsteps, no sounds of anyone moving about in the other rooms. The villa was deathly quiet, and she knew at once that she was alone in it.

Alexandra sat up slowly. She had left her clothes in wild chaos all over the floor, exactly as they had been when she had so eagerly let him undress her. Now they were folded neatly and laid over a chair. His had gone—presumably with him inside them, but he had not left hurriedly. Quietly, stealthily, he had ensured that he did not wake her. Why? Because he did not want to talk about what had happened? Because already he was regretting it?

Her own nakedness suddenly made her blush, and she struggled into a bathrobe. She had given herself with such willing, thoughtless abandon, he could have been in no doubt how much she wanted him. She had never paused to think—how could she have thought at all, in the grip of such a reckless passion?—that this was a man who only a few days earlier had expressed to her his intention of marrying a girl for entirely unromantic reasons. And yet last night had been like a sweet, crazy dream, with both of them carried away on to a plane of wild exultation.

A wave of bitterness swept over her. He had wanted her, too, but he had come to her in a state of relieved exhaustion, light-headed from the burden of worry only just lifted from him. Would any compliant female he found tolerably attractive have served the same purpose? Had he looked at her, this morning when he woke, and thought, good lord, what have I done?

Clinging desperately to a modicum of already fading hope, Alexandra got out of bed and prowled the villa, telling herself that perhaps he had left her a note. There was no note. A man did not write notes to tell a woman, sorry, I shouldn't have slept with you last night, it didn't mean anything!

She showered and washed her hair, put on a navy and white sleeveless dress and white sandals, still straining to hear his key turning in the lock, although by now she was deadly certain he would not come back. At nine o'clock, biting her lip with anxiety, she went along to Reception, dreading the moment when she would have to face him and see in his eyes the confirmation of the awful mistake he felt he had made.

But it was Chantal's sleek blonde head she saw bent over the mail. She looked up and smiled brightly at Alexandra. '*Bonjour*. I hear it is you I have to thank for keeping things ticking.'

'My pleasure,' Alexandra said dully. 'How's the ankle?'

'Oh, it is a little painful, but improving. I can walk only slowly, but no matter.' She slit open another letter and scanned it quickly and expertly before putting it on to one of several piles in front of her. Alexandra's eyes darted over the other woman's shoulder, trying to see if Dominic was in the office.

'If you're looking for Dominic, he was here, very early—I think he must have been up with the larks. But he's gone out, now,' Chantal informed her.

By now, Alexandra was sure beyond any doubt that she was the last person Dominic would want to see. Last night for him had been an aberration, and she thought that, knowing her capacity for emotional involvement, he was afraid that she would not be able to view it with such detachment. And he was right. Still stunned by the experience, she did not know what words to use to describe the ecstasy they had shared.

She only knew it had overtuned her life, leaving no part of it the same.

Chantal was still calmly opening the mail, as if this was just a day like any other.

'Did. . .did Dominic leave any message for me?' Alexandra asked faintly.

'*Comment?* Oh, no, not really. He said there was no need for you to work any more, that's all. Is there a problem?'

'No problem,' Alexandra said quietly, turning away from the counter.

No problem. It was all abundantly clear. Dominic's life, his plans, his feelings had been changed not one iota by the night they had spent together. He still intended to go ahead with his marriage to Nathalie— why not? I'm just a woman he inadvertently slept with, Alexandra thought wretchedly. Perhaps he was afraid that she would think that gave her the right to make demands on him—that she would go on making emotional demands on him, even after he was married. Like mother, like daughter! Was that why he was so carefully avoiding her this morning, beginning, already, the delicate process of distancing himself from her?

Alexandra hurried back to the villa and swiftly thrust clothes and belongings into her case. She was trying very hard not to give in to tears, but it was costing her heavily in iron self-control. Last night had happened, and, no matter what, *she* could not regret it. She had wanted him from the beginning, way back when they were very young, and perhaps the conclusion had been inevitable. But, for him, she had only satisfied a sexual need of the moment—he did not want her in the same way.

Well, she understood the message. Her services were no longer required, and she would not hang around to embarrass him. He need have no fear that she would ask anything more from him, or that she would continue to haunt him, as her mother had haunted his father, for the rest of their lives.

In this day and age, a woman was every bit as entitled to a one-night stand as her male counterpart, and if she left now without fuss, without reproach, he could breathe again, believing that that was all it had been for her. And she would never come back.

She would have liked to leave without seeing anyone, but she had to hand in her key at Reception and meet Chantal's surprised, questioning eyes. 'You're leaving now? Does Dominic know?'

It's none of your damn business, she wanted to shout, whether Dominic knows or not. Are you his watchdog? But she only said politely, 'We've discussed it. He knows I have to get back to Oxford, and only delayed my departure to help him over a difficult spell. I'm considerably behind with my own work.'

Chantal still looked doubtful, but Alexandra wasn't giving her a chance to suggest consulting her employer—wherever he was! '*Au revoir*—I've a train to catch,' she said, and hurried out to the car.

She said *au revoir* silently several times that day—to Roussillon Village, as she drove away, to Perpignan as the train pulled out of the station, and to France as the plane took off from Montpellier, thankfully without too much delay. The sun-drenched Languedoc fell away beneath her as they soared above the clouds. And at Gatwick she saw without surprise that it was raining, and winter had truly arrived for her.

She moved back into her own small flat and into the swim of academic life, and found that Oxford held no terrors for her. She could walk past Tristan's flat, she could visit places she had been with him, with relative equanimity. She had not forgotten, nor would she forget. She had loved him—or thought she had loved him—and now he was gone, and his ghost no longer clung to her as she went about her everyday life. She could function.

During her first week back, before she even gave a thought to getting on with her own work, she sat down and finally discharged the duty she had set herself; the sorting out and editing of Tristan's last poems. She was able to read them now with a clear, unclouded mind, reality no longer distorted by the fog of emotion, and she admitted without rancour that much of Dominic's criticism was apt. They read well enough, but their interest was more in the nature of a postscript to his earlier work, particularly now that publication would be posthumous. There was very little that was new, exciting or of great value with regard to the content.

She remembered how angry and distraught she had been when she had quarrelled with Dominic on this very subject. It seemed unbelievable now that emotional bias could have so clouded her own judgement, and it was as if she looked back at that nerve-racked, disorientated young woman from a great distance. In that sense, at least, her trip to France had been significant, she thought wryly. She had come to terms with Tristan's death, and could finally put it behind her. But at what cost?

Because it had not happened as she had firmly, if a little desperately, told herself it would. She was safely out of reach of Dominic's pervasive charm, his powerful physical charisma, but none of her feelings for him had begun to fade. She thought about him every day when she awoke, and throughout the day he continued to haunt her, until she lay in bed at night, still remembering his touch, his voice, still seeing his face, his eyes—harsh, laughing, cynical, every aspect of him she had ever known.

It will go, she promised herself, with as much faith as she could muster. Give it time. It can't possibly remain as painful, as intense as this indefinitely. You'll get over him. Of course you will. You got over Tristan.

But Dominic was alive. Alive and planning to marry a golden-haired slip of a girl with violet eyes and a deceptively demure smile. For the rest of her life, Alexandra would have to endure this knowledge; she would have to remember that he had rejected her not once, but twice.

Dutifully she made an appointment with Tristan's publisher and took along the edited poems, neatly typed and presented in a slim folder.

'Interesting,' said the nonchalant young man she had spoken to on her last visit. 'Yes, I suppose there might be a small market, if only out of curiosity. Dead poets attract more interest than live ones.'

Alexandra was beginning to dislike him intensely. She was sorely tempted to pick up the folder and say, thank you very much, she would try another publisher, when he said unexpectedly, 'You do realise, of course, that this work constitutes part of the estate of Tristan Carteret, and, as such, any payment or royalties might possibly be claimed by his former wife. She might certainly be inclined to contest.'

And a nice, juicy battle about ownership would be guaranteed to boost sales, Alexandra thought distastefully.

'I hadn't given the matter any thought,' she said curtly. 'Certainly, I don't want or expect to receive any money from it. I just want to see the poems published, and that's my only interest.'

He looked surprised and a little crestfallen. 'I thought we might have a problem there, so I felt obliged to contact Mrs Carteret through her solicitor when I knew you were coming up. She expressed a wish to see you. In fact, she's in the ante-room now.'

Alexandra's heart leapt with foreboding, recalling that distraught, wild-eyed woman hurling abuse at her at Tristan's graveside.

'I'd really rather not meet her,' she said quickly, but he only smiled, as if her preference was of no importance.

'Oh, you must spare her five minutes,' he said unctuously, no doubt still hoping that a meeting would stimulate argument as to whom the poems morally belonged to. 'She's come a long way. Tell you what—I'll leave the two of you alone for a short while, and get my secretary to send in some coffee.'

Knowing full well that there are matters between Mrs Carteret and myself which cannot be solved by a cup of coffee, Alexandra thought sourly. But there seemed to be no honourable way out of this encounter, and, she told herself, she had promised to stop running away from things she found unpleasant. So she allowed him to show her into the ante-room, fully prepared for another distasteful scene.

The woman who faced her bore little resemblance to

the screaming virago at the funeral. Helen Carteret wore a neat grey suit which, although it was clean and smartly pressed, looked as though she had owned it for some time. Her hair was cut short and tidy in a trouble-free style that wouldn't demand too many expensive visits to the hairdressers. Her make-up was out of date, her eyes tired, but she was smiling, bravely and apprehensively.

'Miss Warner.'

'Mrs Carteret.' Alexandra was wary, nevertheless.

'I wanted to meet you again, because. . .' She faltered and then went on, quickly, obviously afraid that if she stopped she would be unable to say what was on her mind '. . .because I felt so bad about the way I behaved at the funeral. Whatever must you have thought of me? I don't usually go off like that, I can assure you.'

Indeed, Alexandra thought, surprised, the virago seemed as timid as a mouse today. Remembering how uptight and nervously stretched she herself had been on the day of the funeral, she realised that Tristan's former wife had been beside herself with stress and anguish, not fully aware of, or in control of what she was saying. She could not bear any resentment towards her.

'Please. . .it's all forgotten, as far as I'm concerned,' she said. 'It was a truly dreadful day, and I can well imagine how you must have felt.'

Mrs Carteret gave a faint, wan smile. 'I had no business feeling anything,' she said. 'Tristan and I split up years earlier, and I was a fool to have gone on loving him. Oh, it was very fine to begin with—promising young poet, and all that. But something went wrong—he couldn't write any more, and he started blaming me, and drinking a lot.'

Alexandra looked sharply at her. This was the woman Tristan claimed had dried him up, 'emasculated' his verse, but her story sounded terribly similar to Alexandra's own. And Helen had endured years of this torment, not just months.

'But you stayed with him for a long time, in spite of everything,' she said curiously. 'You must have loved him very much.'

'I did. I badly wanted to have children, you see, but Tristan thought I shouldn't need a family when I was married to a great poet! If I'd gone ahead and left him while I was still young enough to meet someone else, my life might have been very different. But Tristan would always get me to change my mind, he would beg me to stay. . .say he couldn't manage without me. . .'

I heard that one, too, Alexandra thought, a weary realisation growing within her. She looked at Tristan's ex-wife, and felt a strange sense of sisterhood. 'You divorced him eventually, though,' she observed.

Helen straightened her shoulders and gave a little, practical smile. 'Every worm finally turns,' she said. 'What I couldn't take was his continuous progression of college girls. I didn't see why I should put up with all his tantrums and torments, while some dewy-eyed young graduate sat at his feet in adoration.'

Alexandra gasped sharply, and Helen Carteret bit her lip.

'My dear child—I'm sorry. I shouldn't have said that,' she apologised. 'Hadn't you realised that you were not the first? He liked clever young women who could do his drudgery for him. But I want you to know that I bear you no ill will. We were both Tristan's victims.'

'So it would appear,' Alexandra said quietly, and, somewhere inside the still centre of her brain, she clearly heard Dominic's caustic voice saying he had merely used her to shore up his own inadequacies. What an idiot I was to fall for all that, she thought. How pathetically innocent I must have been.

The secretary brought in coffee, and Helen smiled nervously at Alexandra as she poured. 'Did *you* love him?' she asked.

'I honestly believed so, at the time,' Alexandra said thoughtfully. 'Now I'm not so sure I wasn't deceiving myself, or, to put it more kindly, allowing myself to be deceived.'

She set down her cup, and suddenly it was very clear what she must do. 'The poems are yours, Mrs Carteret,' she said. 'I'm handing them over, not to the publisher, but to you, to do with as you see fit. He was your husband, once, and it seems to me that if they belong to anyone, they belong to you.'

She thought there were tears in the other woman's eyes, but could not be sure, and she hoped Helen's solicitor would help her procure a decent advance. From her appearance, Alexandra could divine that Tristan had not left her well endowed financially. He had taken her youth, and by the time he was through with her the marriage market and the employment market were probably closed doors. Poetry sales were notoriously paltry, but one never knew, and if they helped this sad, tired-looking woman even a little, all *she* had endured at Tristan's hands would not have been entirely futile.

Alexandra left the publisher's office feeling strangely light, floating rather than walking. The last of the shackles had fallen from her, and she was free. No longer was she impelled by guilt to deny what she must have known, inwardly, for some time past—that it was Dominic she loved.

What else had drawn her back to Château Albigny if not the subconscious echoes of a love which had never really died, merely gone underground? Why had she been unable to keep away from him, so quick to be hurt, elated, enraged by anything he said to her? So saddened by the scars of bitter experience which had left him so untrusting and cynical?

And could she have given herself to him so readily, and with such certainty, if something inside her had not known, in spite of her denials, that this *was* love— body, heart and soul combined, as they should be?

She did not understand why it should give her the slightest satisfaction to be able to admit this, at last. Dominic was not in love with her, and she had certainly lost him. She could not return to Château Albigny, since he had made it so plain that he did not want her around any more. She should be miserable, and she had an awful presentiment that she was going to be, soon enough. But, just for today, if only for a few hours, it was sufficient to be certain of what love really was.

For a while she nursed this outrageous, delightful fantasy that he would turn up on her doorstep, having traced her through her college, declaring that after she had gone he had realised he couldn't live without her. Lowering her sights a little, she contemplated a more modest dream in which he arrived saying he was just passing through, and could they have dinner together. . .after which he would realise how much he needed her. Neither came true, of course, and finally she consigned them to the dusty attic of forlorn hopes, where they belonged, and concentrated her attention firmly on her three Victorian poets.

Christmas came, and tentatively she sent a card to the château with her best wishes to everyone. Back came one from Tante Corinne, on behalf of the entire clan, and a pathetic little note from Danielle saying, 'You beast, Lexi, to disappear again so quickly! How could you do that before we had chance to get to know one another again? Please write back to your friend, Dani.'

Alexandra smiled wistfully. She would have loved to correspond regularly with Danielle, but she was sure to mention her brother, and there were things that Alexandra did not want to hear. She did *not* want to hear about his engagement, or to receive photographs of his wedding, or—horrors—an invitation to it! She could only hope that Danielle would not be too hurt by her silence—after all, she had her husband and child, and a full life of her own.

She sent no Christmas greeting exclusively to Dominic, and he sent none to her. The festive season passed, and, as she had known it would, the brief, uplifting glow love had conferred on her faded to a dream. The pain of missing him did not fade; she carried it inside her every day of her life as the long, hard winter dragged to a close, melting finally into a late and chilly spring.

Alexandra had worked hard and unremittingly on her thesis, and by the middle of May it was finished and ready to present. A PhD thesis had to break new ground, to say something about its subject which had not been said before, or at least to slant a fresh light on it. She had sifted through the mounds of learned appreciation and the pages of insubstantial twaddle written about these three great poets, she had researched their lives, read their own letters and those of others, visited their birthplaces, talked to anyone who had a viewpoint which might add weight.

By the time she had done all this, she felt as if she knew each one of them as intimately as close friends; she stood inside their heads and examined their thoughts. And, out of this melting pot, miraculously, emerged her own personal estimate of their place in the illustrious spectrum of English literature.

She entitled her thesis 'The Speaking Silence—A View of the Romantic Poet in History', and deposited it on her tutor's desk with a resounding thud, and a gleam of wicked achievement in her eyes. She knew she had done it, and, although it would have to be independently assessed, she knew when she saw his face after he had read it that he agreed with her.

And now that it was finished, she felt as empty and metaphorically flat as if she had just given birth. Her thesis was written, and it was good. On the strength of it, a contract for a research fellowship was being drawn up for her to sign, ready to commence at the beginning of the next college term in October. She would have a good salary and her foot on the first rung of the career ladder. Alexandra Warner, MA, PhD. Why didn't she feel more elated?

She knew why. Sheer, unrelenting toil had carried her through the last few months; wrapped up in her work, she had refused to let herself think about Dominic, and, even then, it had taken a lot of determined effort to drive out the invading images and memories. Now she no longer had that barricade to hide behind. She had letters after her name, and the respect of her peers. Very nice. And it wasn't enough. In the speaking silence of her own dreams, the love she needed above everything, and could not have, came back to haunt her.

CHAPTER EIGHT

THE contract sat on the telephone table in Alexandra's flat, where it had been for several days, but she was unable to bring herself to sign it. Oxford had been her life for several years, but did she really want to commit herself to this ivory tower world, with its fierce internal intrigues and concentrated air of learning, for a further period?

It occurred to her that she would rather be out in the world at large, among the commercial cut and thrust, but all she seemed able to do was to contemplate the alternatives and come to no firm decision. Teaching? She did not really have the motivation to teach. Publishing. . . PR. . .what else could a first-class arts graduate do? Business? She had enjoyed her few days in the office at Roussillon Village. . .something travel-related? She spoke excellent French. It was unfair to keep the college authorities waiting on her decision, so she would have to make her mind up soon.

It was while she was dithering thus that the invitation arrived. Printed in gilt on a little vellum card, it announced that Corinne d'Albigny was having a celebration to mark the occasion of her seventy-fifth birthday, and Alexandra Warner's presence was formally requested. At the bottom of the card the old lady had written simply, 'Please come.'

Alexandra stood gazing out of the window of her flat, the card in her hand. Below, in the park across the road, the cherry trees were bursting into blossom. Bicycling students whizzed past en route to their lectures, as they had done for years, and in the distance Matthew Arnold's 'dreaming spires' crested the skyline. She saw all this, but did not register it, because in her mind she was seeing acres of vines springing from the terracotta earth, under a brilliant sun, beneath the snow-capped shadow of Mount Canigou. Seeing the man she loved, her cousin Dominic, brushing back the dark hair from his scarred temple and smiling his cynical, dazzling smile.

She couldn't go. It would hurt too much, for one thing, seeing him again. Lord knew, it still hurt, after all these months. Where was the sense in ripping the barely healed skin from the wound and causing the blood to flow fresh and painfully again? Besides, wouldn't he think, it's started—here was this woman, all set to cause emotional chaos in his life, just as her mother had done to his father, instead of leaving well alone?

But Tante Corinne wanted her to be there, and those two short words appended to the card barely disguised an appeal it was hard to refuse. She was a creaking gate, healthwise; she was seventy-five, and this was a birthday she might well not have seen. How could Alexandra turn her down? She looked at the calendar, saw that the proposed date was only two weeks away, and sighed deeply.

When it came right down to it, she did not have a great deal of choice. It was not even a matter of what she herself wanted, or what Dominic would have preferred. Being part of a family, as she had wanted to be, conferred responsibilities as well as benefits.

Among its unwritten rules was the prime consideration of not hurting or disappointing those who cared for you. Alexandra sent off a little note to Tante Corinne, thanking her for the invitation, and indicating that she would be pleased to attend. Then she went to book her flight.

'That's the second time in a year you've been to southern France, isn't it?' said the chatty young clerk at the travel agent's, remembering her from her visit the previous October.

'Yes. I have relatives there,' replied Alexandra, who had just bought Tante Corinne's present, an exquisite shawl of white Nottingham lace. Simply making the claim gave her a pleasant little glow of belonging.

'Lucky for some! Well, at least the summer schedules are in operation now, and you'll be able to fly direct to Perpignan.'

The very mention of the city where she had spent those memorable days in Dominic's apartment set Alexandra's legs trembling, and she emerged from the travel agent's with a bad case of the jitters. Were it not for Tante Corinne, she knew she should not go back, but she could not deny that there would be secret delights along with the agonies of this visit. It was pointless to pretend that she wasn't counting the minutes until she saw Dominic again. Much good it would do her!

A few days later, out of the blue, a letter arrived bearing a French stamp. She did not recognise the writing. It wasn't Tante Corinne's, and it certainly wasn't Dominic's. Quickly she slit the envelope and took out a sheet of faintly perfumed lilac paper.

A DREAM TOO SWEET

My dear Alexandra,
I have had cause to regret that we did not meet when you were here last October, and I am so glad you will be coming for the birthday celebrations. It would give me great pleasure if you would stay as my guest while you are here. I should be delighted to have your company, and the chance to get to know you a little.

If you accept my invitation—and I hope you will—please let me know the time of your flight so I can meet you at the airport.

Françoise d'Albigny.

Why was it, Alexandra wondered with a little smile, that all invitations from the d'Albigny family sounded suspiciously like royal commands? But this was Dominic's mother, the only one of the clan who had remained reluctant to bury the past, and she was now holding out a hand to Alexandra. She would have been a fool had she failed to take it.

Tante Françoise had added as a postscript:

I don't suppose anyone has thought to mention to you the important matter of dress! My usual attire these days is jeans and a paint-splattered smock, but lurking somewhere at the back of my wardrobe is the obligatory little black cocktail dress. I assume you have something similar.

Alexandra chuckled. There was a dry wit behind the words that reminded her of Dominic, but she sobered as she recalled that this woman was the last surviving third of that disastrous triangle of love, years ago. It would be impossible to meet her without thinking of that. However, she had issued the invitation herself, so surely it would be all right?

As to dress, the only halfway formal occasions Alexandra had attended recently were the dean's sherry parties, and she wasn't about to face Dominic and a château full of local gentry and worthies, including Nathalie Paulin—who would certainly look divine—without the morale-booster of a new dress! Oxford had some good, if expensive boutiques, and she was all set to dispose of whatever she had saved from her grant during a very frugal and unsocial winter.

It's the employment agencies for you, my girl, the minute you get back, she told herself grimly. Meanwhile—hang the expense!

Françoise d'Albigny, true to her word, was waiting to meet Alexandra when she arrived at the airport the day before the party. Although in her fifties, Dominic's mother still had the trim, slim figure of a girl, and her arrow-straight carriage, the dark hair springing back in a loose wave from her temples, her firm, aquiline nose, were all poignant reminders of him.

Alexandra had bitten her nails to the quick during the flight in nervous anticipation of this meeting, but the moment Françoise kissed her warmly on both cheeks and smiled directly into her eyes she wondered why she had been at all apprehensive.

'There's no mistaking who you are,' Françoise said, and then, echoing Alexandra's own thoughts, 'You know, I was afraid to meet you before. I thought it would hurt, because Dominic told me how like *her* you were—like Christine. But it doesn't—not at all.'

Alexandra's smile was sincere, but puzzled. 'All of

you tell me that I'm like my mother, but I think time must be playing tricks on you,' she said ruefully. 'She was so beautiful.'

'And you think you are not?' Françoise asked gently. 'Christine was beautiful, yes, one cannot deny that. But her beauty was more. . .conventional. You have something different, something that will linger in the mind. It comes and goes. . .when you smile, or turn your head. Yours is a face I should like to paint, if you would permit it.'

'I would be honoured,' Alexandra said. 'But I don't think I can stay very long, Tante Françoise.'

'Oh, please. . .you can drop the "Tante". You are a big girl, now, and it makes me feel ancient!' Dominic's mother laughed. 'And do stay as long as you wish. It will be my pleasure.'

She led Alexandra to a nippy little white Peugeot, and soon they were bowling along the main road. The sun was hot and bright, the mountains were clear and blue in the near distance; seawards, the long, thin line of the coastal *étangs* shimmered lapis lazuli. Alexandra sighed, relishing the warmth, the brilliance, the sheer, exuberant beauty of the Roussillon, and wished it did not feel so much like coming home. It would make leaving so very much harder.

Françoise drove quickly out along the Prades road. Inland, away from the racing development of the coastal strip, very little had changed in years. The mountains loomed closer, little rushing streams splashed under tiny stone bridges, dusty tracks led to the occasional isolated house, lost in a sea of vines which grew wherever land was cultivable.

After a while Alexandra saw perched high on a

hillside the most enchanting village. It seemed to grow up the steep slope, the crumbling, golden stone houses perched virtually on the shoulders of those below, crowned by the tower of a church at the very top.

'That's the village where I live,' Françoise said.

It looked very near, but the terrain was so hilly, the narrow road climbed, dipped, and rose yet again in hairpin bends. Françoise manoeuvred the car around these tight corners with the deftness born of long practice, but Alexandra shuddered at the sheer drops which fell away at the side of the road, giving sudden, terrifying views of the valley far below. Across it, the mighty shoulder of Canigou reared dizzyingly, casting a giant shadow, and the old mountain gods seemed very real and powerful, waiting for these foolhardy mortals to make one small slip.

At last they reached the lower part of the village, where there was parking space for cars.

'We must walk the rest of the way,' Françoise said, and Alexandra was quite thankful to get out and proceed on foot. She followed her hostess along tiny pathways, leading higher and yet deeper into the village, so narrow that in places the buildings met overhead, creating a tunnel. Little alleys became flights of crumbling steps, where she caught occasional glimpses along dark passages into cool, dim houses and walled gardens profuse with greenery.

They traversed a square, in the centre of which was a stone trough and a pump, and Françoise laughed. 'Very picturesque, but it's not so very long since the women of the village used to do their washing here,' she said, pausing for breath. All was quiet, there wasn't a soul around, and Alexandra could have believed that the village was deserted.

Françoise assured her that this was an illusion. 'People will be watching us. Villages are like that. You are a stranger, and they're by no means sure of me, yet. I've only been here a few years!'

She led Alexandra along yet another narrow passageway, and finally opened the door of a small house, secretive and enclosed like so many of its neighbours.

'As you can see, it isn't very big,' she said. 'Upstairs there are just two tiny bedrooms and a shower-room. My paintings take up much of the ground floor. But most of the time I am on my own, and I find it refreshing not to have the worry of a large house. And, of course, in this climate we live much of our lives outdoors on the *terrasse*.'

It was in truth not very spacious. There was a minimum of furniture of an almost Spartan plainness, and this, Alexandra reminded herself, was a woman who had lived many years in the grandeur of Château Albigny. It was hard to avoid the conclusion that Françoise had consciously and deliberately reacted against it.

Canvases were stacked around the walls on every available inch of space, and one in progress took pride of place on an easel. There were views of the mountains and the village from different aspects, painted in spring and in autumn, in full sunlight or in the gathering dusk, mysterious with shadows. Portraits, too—weather-beaten village women and wrinkled old men, earthy and full of life.

'These are wonderful!' Alexandra exclaimed, setting

down her suitcase and gazing around her. 'You are really talented—I had no idea.'

Françoise smiled with shy pleasure. 'Do you think so? I took it up more as a kind of therapy, something to do, than with any serious intent. I always enjoyed painting as a girl, but then I got married, and I never thought of it again until I came to live here. Come and see my inspiration.'

Alexandra stepped out on to the terrace, and gave a little cry. Below them were the crazily angled roof-tops of the village, the road snaking down to the plain far below. From here, the view was clear and uninterrupted across the valley to Canigou. It looked so close she felt she could almost reach out and touch the great, green, purple-shadowed flanks.

'It would make an artist of anyone with the slightest inclination that way,' Françoise said, and Alexandra could not disagree.

They sat in comfortable old wicker chairs, drinking chilled white wine and eating salad, crusty bread and fresh peaches, all prepared in advance by Françoise.

'This place has been so good for me,' she confided. 'It restored my sanity, and my faith in myself. I had a severe nervous breakdown, after. . .well, you know. Did Dominic tell you that?'

'No, he didn't,' Alexandra said slowly. She had sensed his protectiveness where his mother was concerned, but had never known the full reason for it. Now she understood a little better.

Françoise's smile faded, her face was grave as she continued her story. 'Oh, yes, for many months I had no idea what I was doing, or even what time of day it was. I existed in a kind of haze, stuffed full of tranquillisers. It was really Dominic who held the family together. Matthieu was withdrawn and bitter; he no longer had the will to be a concerned father. His mother was very ill for a long time. So Dominic would come home at weekends, all the way from his studies at the Sorbonne in Paris, to help Michel and the girls. He would talk to them about their problems and encourage them with their schoolwork.'

She could not suppress a little sigh. 'It was a lot to ask of a young man who would normally have been enjoying a full social life in his free time. I often think that it made him grow up too quickly. He had to take on responsibilities too heavy, too young, and he still bears the scars.'

Alexandra was quiet. If only she had known the full extent of this family's sufferings earlier, she could have understood better the resentment, the wariness she had encountered on her last visit. Understood, too, what had helped make Dominic the way he was today, a man determined at all costs to maintain his armour-plated emotional detachment.

In a low, careful voice, she said, 'If I'd had any idea what had happened in the past, I would never have come back. My only defence is that I acted in complete ignorance.'

Françoise touched her hand reassuringly. 'You need no defence, and you must not let it trouble you any more. You were just an innocent child when all this took place. Why should you have known, if Christine did not choose to tell you? It was wrong of us, as a family, to reject you as we did.'

Alexandra looked down, trying to fight a hot flush

spreading slowly up her neck. It was fortunate that Françoise did not know that the same 'innocent child' had been in the stables, trying ineptly to entice Dominic to make love to her, at the very moment her mother was in bed with Dominic's father! Had she succeeded, they might well have branded her as a scarlet woman, too!

But she said nothing as Françoise poured more wine.

'I'm glad you're here,' Dominic's mother said. 'Seeing you again has finally made me realise that I'm free. I loved my husband very much, although, when we married, I knew he did not love me. That didn't trouble me too much at the time. I thought that, over the years, with having children, sharing the process of living, what I thought of as a childhood infatuation would be driven from his mind. I thought he would forget Christine and be totally mine.

'It never happened. For a long time I was very angry and bitter, but it's over. I've forgiven them for loving one another, and accepted that perhaps it was beyond their control.'

'That isn't what Dominic thinks,' Alexandra said impulsively. 'According to him, nothing can excuse what they did.'

'Ah. . . Dominic.' Françoise frowned. 'He worries me. He has all the attributes and trappings of an outwardly successful man—prospering business interests, many friends, a different girl every time I see him. But these are not substitutes for a real, lasting love. More than anything, I should like him to find for himself what I never had.'

'I think,' Alexandra ventured cautiously, 'that there is a girl who is perhaps more important than the others.'

Françoise shot her a sharp, perceptive glance. 'I suppose you mean the little Paulin girl?' she said dismissively. 'A manipulative little minx with her eye on the main chance, if you ask me! But she's a child! My son needs a real woman, for, whatever his faults, he's a handful of a man, and he'd soon be bored silly by *that* one! I wish there was something I could do to make him see sense—something anyone could do.'

There was a pleading note in her voice, almost as if she was appealing to Alexandra for help. For a moment Alexandra wondered if she had inadvertently given away something of how she felt. But, surely, even a mother's intuition could not have picked that up so quickly? And even though she loved Dominic, there was nothing she could do. He had only wanted her superficially, and she had no power to influence him.

'He is, as you say, a man, and will do as he pleases,' she said quietly, and thought she surprised a fleeting disappointment on Françoise's face.

Later, as she was unpacking her clothes in the tiny but charming bedroom under the eaves, with a view of the pocket-handkerchief garden of the house below, she heard someone knock on the door.

'*Maman!*' she heard an all too familiar voice call out, and she froze in the process of setting out her cosmetics on the small wooden dresser.

Dominic! Dominic was here—now? She had not expected to have to face him until tomorrow, and by then she would have been as prepared as it was possible to be—hair freshly washed, face carefully made up, in all the expensive, protective glory of her new, designer-label dress. But not now, in her travel-worn jeans and sweatshirt, looking like the Wreck of the Hesperus, she thought wretchedly. What was he doing here? Françoise had not said she was expecting him. Had she known?

'Dominic—*quelle bonne surprise!*' Françoise's happy cry as she opened the door answered that question for her, only to pose others. Why should Dominic choose today to pay his mother an unexpected visit? He must have been aware that she was here. A shiver of unexplained foreboding shook her. He could not be here for the pleasure of seeing her again.

She knew she could not hope to skulk in her bedroom until he left. She had to go down, greet him as pleasantly and casually as one would normally greet one's cousin, behave naturally, smile and chat. But how? The last time she saw this man, they had been naked in one another's arms in the bedroom at Roussillon Village. Yes, it was months ago, but the memory was as painfully fresh as if it had happened only yesterday.

Alexandra pulled a brush through her tangled hair, straightened her shoulders, and carefully negotiated the steep, narrow staircase. And there he was, standing in the living-room, admiring his mother's latest painting. The sunlight streaming in through the windows glinted on the thick, black hair, and the smile faded from his face as he turned towards her. She loved him so much, the pain and joy were like a knife slicing through her as easily as if she were soft, pliant clay, and he looked at her as though she was the last person in the world he wanted to see.

'Hello, Dominic.' She hoped her voice sounded level, with just the correct degree of warmth required, but had no way of judging.

'Alexandra. Did you have a good flight?'

'Not too bad. At least, we took off no more than half an hour late, which is pretty good going these days.'

Superficial chat. Hoping it would carry her through the awfulness of this meeting, trying not to think of the last one. His lips against her throat—'you're beautiful'—no, she must not keep on reliving it.

'It was good of you to come. It means a lot to *Grandmère*.' He spoke to her coolly, without emotion, as one would to a casual acquaintance met on the street.

'It's an important birthday. I couldn't disappoint her.' Her heart was solidified lead inside her, hard and lumpen, but his very words emphasised that her being here, although significant to Tante Corinne, meant nothing to him, and she had to act as if she felt the same way.

Françoise smiled from one to the other of them excessively brightly. 'Why don't you go out on to the *terrasse, mes enfants*? I'll bring some coffee.'

Alexandra accepted with alacrity. Outside, she thought, she would be less overwhelmed by the sheer physical awareness of him, and it would be easier to control her reaction to it. But it did not help a lot. She watched him relax into one of the wicker chairs, found herself studying intently the fine, long-fingered hands, the lithe-limbed elegance of form, the broad shoulders under the casual cotton summer shirt.

She had known this was going to hurt, but she had not been prepared for the intensity of wanting, the raw, primitive need to reach out and touch him, which neither time nor distance had lessened. It was unfair.

'I suppose I must address you as Dr Warner these days?' he asked, with a faintly sarcastic smile, and

Alexandra jumped a little, still unused to the mode of address her PhD had conferred on her. 'Presumably you'll be a fully-fledged don, come October.'

'The university has offered me a contract, but I haven't decided yet whether to accept,' she replied, trying hard to match him in coolness.

'Oh?' The dark eyebrows arched in surprise. 'I thought you had your heart firmly set on the academic life.'

And you'd be relieved to have me ensconced at Oxford, well away from here, she thought bitterly. Seized by a dark, wicked desire not to give him that easy assurance, she said frostily, 'Well, you thought wrong. There are a number of options open to me, and my mind is far from made up. You don't know everything about me.'

'*Bien sûr*, I'm aware that you're full of surprises,' he agreed, and from the sardonic curve of his lips, the disdainful gleam in the depths of his eyes, she knew that he was referring to that night of passionate loving. She looked away from his face, ashamed and sickened. How eager she had been; what a pathetic fool he must have thought her! And yet, if he wanted only to pretend it had never happened, why bring the subject up at all? Was it merely to embarrass her?

Françoise mercifully interrupted the conversation, bustling out with the tray, but Alexandra noted that there were only two cups on it.

'I have to go out for a short while. I hope you don't mind,' she said to Alexandra. 'There's this old lady in the village, Madame Desforges, she hasn't been well, and I've been keeping an eye on her. You don't mind, do you? I'm sure Dominic will entertain you until I get back.'

Alexandra smiled weakly. She could hardly protest, and after Françoise had left a heavy silence fell, which she found oppressive. Dominic sat drinking his coffee, saying nothing, but every now and then she caught him eyeing her strangely, as if something about her enraged and disturbed him.

I'm not here to make trouble, to make demands, she wanted to say, if that's what is worrying you. But. . .it was odd. . .she had the feeling that, if either one of them was to move an inch, that same, primitive desire would drive them into each other's arms. She gripped the arms of her chair fiercely and resisted the waves of angry emotion flowing between them.

Desperate to break the tense silence, she cast around for a subject it was safe to broach, and finally asked, 'Is the family all well?'

'Everyone is fine, thank you.' The dark eyes fixed on her glittered with reproach. 'Danielle expects a new baby early next year. She was disappointed that you did not write to her. It would have cost you little.'

She flinched inwardly at the censure in his voice. It would have cost her a great deal, but she dared not let him know how much. 'I was very tied up with my thesis,' she said lamely.

'Yes. And with Tristan's earth-shattering poetry, no doubt,' he said caustically. 'Is the great work finally launched?'

'You could say that. It's off my hands,' she snapped back, sharply, tension cracking her composure. 'I finished editing it and signed it over to his ex-wife.'

She was rewarded by a long, searching stare, and

suddenly she was back on that memorable afternoon when they had lunched together at Roussillon Village, when she had told him her story. She remembered that unmistakable certainly that he wanted to make love to her, and, once again, her body responded to those same unseen signals.

'I thought, according to you, she was a first-rate bitch,' he said drily. 'Why the change of heart?'

'I was wrong. I make mistakes sometimes, Dominic,' she said quietly. 'Most of us do. It's called being human.'

He got up, swiftly, paced the terrace with long, restless strides, and then turned back to face her. His expression was dark with scorn, and something else. . .something nameless, which made Alexandra tremble with fearful excitement.

'It's called being foolish,' he corrected her icily. 'But then—we all make misjudgements about our fellow men. . .and women.'

Like the one we made that night at the villa, she thought. You thought you could use me for a little light relief; I thought that, because you made love to me, I meant something to you. She tried to shrug it away, lightly. 'We have to put our mistakes behind us, and move on,' she said. 'Didn't you tell me that yourself?'

'Well, you certainly took me literally,' he replied caustically. 'I never expected you to come back—not again.'

'I'm here for Tante Corinne's birthday, that's all,' she insisted.

'Are you quite sure, Alexandra?'

He took a step towards her, and involuntarily, as if jerked by marionette strings, she rose from her chair.

Only inches separated them, and she knew beyond doubt that he wanted her, right now. No! she told herself fiercely, she must not give in to this need. She could feel desire emanating from him, and knew that if she touched him now he would take her, swiftly and ruthlessly.

But he did not love her, and he would hate her afterwards for bringing chaos back into his neatly ordered life. He would turn his back on her, and go ahead with his advantageous marriage to Nathalie Paulin, leaving her with only memories of a few more passionate moments.

She turned her head away, closing her eyes and saying quietly, 'Dominic, I'm quite certain,' wishing she could not feel the warmth of his breath on her neck, wishing a chasm would open up at her feet and rescue her from temptation.

It didn't, but as if in response to her silent plea the golden sky began to darken dramatically, and dense black clouds massed and boiled over the lofty peaks. A spot of rain splashed on the tiled floor between them, then another, and, with the suddenness with which rain could come in Mediterranean lands, it began to pelt.

'We had better go indoors,' he said, releasing her from her tense captivity, and, shaking drops of water from their hair, they retreated to the living-room. As he fastened the windows behind them the sky grew as black as night, for all it was only six-thirty on a June evening, lightning forked across their vision, and a fierce, resonant crash of thunder shook the walls of the house. Within seconds a full-scale thunderstorm was in progress, and the mountains were invisible. All they could see outside was rain driving against the windows.

Dominic lit two oil lamps. 'Trust my mother to go the whole way in her search for the primitive, and buy a house with no electricity,' he said wryly. 'Would you like me to close the shutters?'

Alexandra shook her head. The emotional storm raging inside her was far more frightening than the elemental chaos outside. 'No, thank you. I prefer to see what's happening.'

Just a glimmer of a smile touched his lips. 'You won't see very much, with all that rain. Let's have a drink.'

She thought that that was probably the best suggestion he had made since he arrived, and watched him silently as he poured two cognacs, bringing them over to where she stood by the windows. A little, a very little of the tension left her as they stood side by side, looking out on the watery world.

She turned her head to look up at him, and at the same moment he turned towards her. Something trembled in the air between them, words waiting to be spoken, thoughts needing to be expressed. He reached out and touched her hair, very lightly, rubbing a thin, red-gold strand between thumb and forefinger. She shivered; it was no use, even this infinitesimal contact was enough to destroy her fragile resistance. Her eyes closed, waiting for the touch of his lips...

Then the telephone rang shrilly, cutting into the fraught, sensitive moment. He moved away from her to answer it; she heard him say, 'Yes, *Maman*,' and then, 'Very well, if you wish,' and he put the receiver down.

'It appears Madame Desforges is terrified of thunderstorms,' he said. 'My mother feels obliged to stay with her until the worst has passed. I'm afraid she assumes

I'll stay for dinner. In fact, she expects me to make a start on it.'

'How very unfortunate for you,' Alexandra said sarcastically. She was still in a state of turmoil from the strain of those moments when she had almost been in his arms again, and it did not help to hear him regretting his inability to put as much distance as possible between them. 'Am I about to have the pleasure of seeing the Cooking Comte in action? I thought all those cookery books in your apartment were just there to impress guests.'

'Not at all. I'm an excellent cook,' he said immodestly. 'And I trust you're as able with a Sabatier knife as you are with your tongue, because I shall expect you to help.'

He seemed to have recovered completely from the momentary weakness that had threatened to overcome him, and she hated him for his resolute ability to keep the upper hand over his emotions.

'If you think your mother will trust me in her kitchen, I'll gladly prepare dinner myself,' she retorted swiftly. 'Contrary to what you think, I'm an adequate—if not to say "excellent"—cook, and I'd hate you to feel under any obligation to stay.'

'Alexandra. Look outside. It's a cloudburst,' he said scathingly. 'You must have taken note of the road as you drove up. It's hair-raising enough when it's dry; right now, it will be a quagmire. If you think I'm risking my neck driving down the mountain in this, simply to spare us the necessity of enduring one another's company for an hour or two, then, *ma chérie*, as you say in England—you have another think coming!'

CHAPTER NINE

FRANÇOISE had bought a magnificent sea bass for dinner, and, watching Dominic gut, clean and expertly prepare it in the tiny kitchen, Alexandra could tell he had not been boasting idly about his culinary abilities. He knew about food.

'I wonder where you ever learned to do that,' she said, a little tartly. Being confined with him in so small a space, where there was the constant possibility of their brushing against one another, was not good for her already overstrung nerves. 'In your younger days at Château Albigny, as I seem to remember, food was just something that was put in front of you whenever you required it.'

'I was too fond of the outdoor life, then, to frequent the kitchens,' he said calmly. He seemed to have got a firm grip on himself now, although he avoided looking directly into her eyes and did not touch her more than was absolutely necessary. 'But I worked at a restaurant in Paris, once, during my college vacation. It taught me a good deal about food which I've never forgotten.'

He looked pointedly at her briefly idle hands. 'Don't just stand there asking silly questions. You're supposed to be chopping those vegetables.'

'Perhaps I don't like being delegated all the menial tasks,' she glowered resentfully.

'That's the way it is, *chérie*. Here you are not Dr

Warner, MA, PhD. You're just a commis chef, so, if you want to eat, get on with it.'

Alexandra took out her nervous anger on the onions, sniffing and blinking as their odour made her eyes run. He called her '*chérie*' and '*ma chérie*', but there was heavy irony and no warmth at all in his voice. In fact, he was being deliberately cutting and unpleasant to her, as if he blamed her because, briefly, he had been tempted to make love to her.

She watched him wrap the fish gently in foil, after rubbing it with butter and laying it on a bed of herbs. Outside, the storm raged furiously, rain battered the window, thunder crashed, lightning zig-zagged crazily across the heavens. Here she was, marooned in a house in a mountain village, alone with the man she loved, who did not love her and who wished she was a thousand miles away. They worked together, and yet they were not together; most of the time a cold silence reigned, and anything she said provoked a sarcastic remark or an implied criticism. Inside her, it was as dark as the night outside, a black, black misery, with tears just below the surface.

She finished preparing the vegetables, and tried to distract herself from her wretchedness by laying the small dining table with china and glasses she found in the cupboards. There were candles, too, and she set two of them in pottery candlesticks, moving a vase of wild flowers to the table to serve as a centre-piece, making the whole as attractive as she could. There was no Spode or Limoges or crystal here; the crockery was traditional earthenware, the glasses the kind of plain goblets one found in use in bars and cafés.

'Very pretty,' he said unsmilingly, emerging from the

kitchen and surveying her handiwork with a jaundiced eye. 'It's not a festive occasion, you know. You didn't need to go to any trouble. And I do hope you aren't thinking my mother is short of money. She could very easily afford better.'

'It may not be a festive occasion for *you*, but I'm your mother's guest, and I want to repay her kindness in any small way I can,' she retorted coldly. 'Furthermore, I understand perfectly that everything here is a. . .a statement of personal change. . .almost of rebirth.'

He raised his eyebrows in sardonic interrogation, and, although it was difficult to proceed with him staring at her so sceptically, Alexandra was obliged to continue.

'She left the château, and with it all the fine things she equated with unhappiness,' she said quietly. 'It must have taken courage to start again, alone, at her age. I think your mother is a remarkable woman, and I like her very much.'

'Yes, you seem to have inveigled your way into her affections,' he said drily. 'However, I should warn you against overstaying your welcome. You'd do well to remember the old Spanish proverb—guests and fish stink after the third day.'

She gasped. 'How dare you? I think the length of my stay is a matter between your mother and myself, and I'll thank you to keep your unwanted advice to yourself.'

She saw the mask of cold detachment slip, briefly, and fury leapt in his eyes. His hands clenched, and for a wild moment she thought he was going to take hold of her and shake her. Yes, *do* that, please, she willed him silently, despising herself for wanting his hard, angry touch, even if it hurt. She never knew if he would have restrained himself or not, for the door burst open and Françoise rushed in, stripping off her dripping mac and shaking her umbrella.

'It's raining—how do you say?—cats and dogs out there,' she announced unnecessarily. 'But at least the thunder has moved away a little, so it does not sound quite so loud. I think Madame Desforges will be all right on her own now.'

Her smile broadened as she sniffed the air appreciatively. 'Oh, you good children! It smells as if dinner is well on the way, already,' she congratulated them, ignoring their sullen, angry faces. 'There is very little left for me to do.'

'Your son fancies himself as the next Raymond Blanc. I just did the labouring,' Alexandra informed her humourlessly.

'Ah, but the table looks *charmante*! I imagine you are responsible for that. Dominic, open the wine, please. This is lovely! I haven't had two guests at the same time in ages!'

The food was marvellous, the fish cooked just to the point where the flesh fell away at the touch of a knife; the cream sauce, delicately flavoured with vermouth, was exquisite. Otherwise, the meal was a penance. Françoise talked a lot, in the manner of one who lived alone and had to take the opportunity when it came— and it was a good thing she did, because neither of her fellow diners was in the mood for conversational brilliance.

Alexandra did her best to be polite and sociable, but it was hard, with Dominic sitting opposite her replying only monosyllabically to anything she said. His antagonism came at her in waves so strong she felt she was fighting them for breath.

Well, she had known when she accepted the invitation that he would not welcome her, but there was nothing she could do until after the party. This visit was for Tante Corinne, and Alexandra did not see how she could have refused to be present. But there would be no more, not even if it meant losing touch once again, this time finally, with her newly rediscovered family. If her resolve wavered, she had only to look at Dominic's dark, closed face to renew her determination.

After the fish, there was a splendid choux pastry ring stuffed with chocolate and nuts which Françoise had made, more wine, and then coffee.

'Have another cognac, Dominic,' his mother urged him. 'You cannot possibly drive back tonight, in this weather, so what does it matter? The road will be impassable.'

He held out his glass, accepting the obvious wisdom of this. 'True. But I can't stay here. You have only the two bedrooms, both of which will be occupied,' he observed pointedly, every remark calculated to make Alexandra feel more unwelcome.

'There is always the couch,' Françoise said.

'*Maman*, I'm six feet two. Do you want me to develope permanent curvature of the spine?' he said. 'Don't worry—I'll go to the *auberge* opposite the church. They are sure to have a room.'

It was still raining, although less violently, when he took his leave, kissing both his mother and Alexandra on both cheeks. It was accepted French custom between family and close friends, and it would have looked odd if Alexandra had evaded his brief embrace. But the touch of his hands on her shoulders, the lingering hint of Aramis which remained with her after his lips brushed her cheek, left her shaken and faint with longing.

She lay in her narrow bed in the tiny room under the steeply pitched roof, listening to the rain and thinking about him. Wondering if he, too, was awake and listening to it in his room at the *auberge*.

But why should he be? Although she knew he had felt the current of attraction running strongly between them, he was not in love with her. His only fear was that she might stay to make demands on him he did not wish to meet. He might find that irritating and inconvenient, but she did not think it would prevent him from sleeping soundly in his bed.

It took her a long time to get to sleep, and the next thing she knew Françoise was tapping lightly on her door.

'Alexandra! Are you awake?'

Alexandra sat up, brushing her hair from her eyes, as Françoise entered carrying a tray with coffee and delicious-smelling croissants. Setting the tray on the bedside table, she flung open the shutters to admit a brilliant morning, sky and mountains washed clean, not a cloud or a hint of rain anywhere.

'Gracious—what time is it?' Alexandra asked sleepily, and Françoise laughed.

'Almost ten. I looked in earlier, but you were fast asleep. You must have been worn out. Dominic left a while ago—I saw him when I went to fetch the croissants. The road is manageable now, with care, and he is a good driver.'

'I never meant to sleep this late!' Alexandra said guiltily. 'You should have woken me.'

'*Pourquoi?* There is no plane to catch today. This morning, I plan to take you to Villefranche le Confluent, if you would like. It is a small fortified town, very picturesque, which I think you will find interesting. Then we shall have all afternoon to make ourselves beautiful for the party.'

They spent a pleasant day, at ease in one another's company. Villefranche le Confluent was a perfectly preserved medieval town, ringed by towering, protective walls, and set in spectacular mountain scenery. After a leisurely stroll around the ramparts, admiring splendid views in every direction, they ate lunch in the courtyard of a delightful restaurant before driving back to the village.

All the while Alexandra was conscious of the approaching evening, and, happy as she would be to see Tante Corinne and the rest of the family, the thought of Dominic plunged her into despair.

If only they could part friends, she would be. . .well, not content, never that, but at least she would not have to leave with the sour taste of his hatred poisoning her life. If only she could make him see that she wished him well, and did not intend to plague him.

She was glad she had splashed out on the expensive dress when the time came to get ready. There was no room for a full-length mirror in her minute bedroom, so she surveyed herself critically in the one in Françoise's room, and had to admit that she looked good.

The slim white skirt was just about knee length, and the neatly fitted black bodice was Spanish-inspired, with buttons from throat to waist, where it flared into a peplum. She had bought it from one of those shops where nothing had price tags, and if you needed to ask what it cost you probably could not afford it, but she had been persuaded to try it on by two salesgirls who obviously adored everything they sold.

'Perfect!' Françoise gave it her astute Frenchwoman's seal of approval. '*Bon chic*. It has drama and subtlety, both together—a formidable combination. And it fits you like a glove.'

Rather too much like a glove, Alexandra thought nervously. The fashionable length showed off her long, slim legs, the peplum hugged her waist, and the bodice, while revealing not an inch of her, emphasised the firm line of her breasts. In a dress like this one had to walk straight and tall, ashamed of nothing, and consciously she breathed in deeply, adjusting her posture. Françoise had miraculously tamed her gleaming but unruly hair into a sophisticated French plait, secured by gold clips, and had insisted on lending her a pair of gold and pearl drop earrings to complete the effect.

Françoise herself wore black, too: a timelessly elegant dress of brocade overlaid by fine lace. 'We shall be belles of the ball,' she said brightly, and then gave a sudden grimace. 'To tell the truth, I am nervous. I am not used to these grand events, nowadays; I keep telling myself it is only a birthday party for my *belle-mère*, but I know everyone who is anyone will be there.'

Alexandra squeezed her hand. 'I'm nervous, too,' she confided.

'You? But why? You are young and lovely, and all the young men will swoon over you.'

'I'm not used to grand events at all. Nor to men swooning over me.'

'This I find hard to believe,' said Dominic's mother. 'I think perhaps you have been hiding your light, and your powers are only half tested. Or perhaps you are a woman who needs one certain man, and then—pouf!' She imitated a rocket exploding.

Perhaps, like you, like my mother, I'm a woman with a talent for loving the wrong man, Alexandra thought. Maybe Dominic was right after all, and it did run in the family!

They arrived just as the sun was sinking below the rim of the mountains and the château was magnificently ablaze. Lights shone from every window, the rosy stone glowed in the last reflection of the sunset, and the lovely gardens had been artistically floodlit for the occasion. People were walking on the terrace and in the gardens, the men suave and elegant in dark suits, the women's gowns a brilliant array of fashion in a rainbow of colours and gorgeous materials.

In the huge formal dining-room a splendid buffet was set out, with servants waiting to help dispense it, while others moved among the guests with crystal flutes of chilled champagne on silver trays. In the grand salon a trio of musicians played softly, the sound drifting out into the hall where Tante Corinne, her silver-streaked hair piled high on her head in a fashion of bygone years, sat in her wheelchair, elegant in a grey silk gown. Her eyes sparkled with a revived enthusiasm for life, and she kissed Alexandra warmly as she accepted her gift.

'How sweet of you to come all this way for an old lady,' she said, but her queenly manner belied the humility of the words, Alexandra thought, smiling. 'And I never had the chance to thank you for helping Dominic when I was taken ill.'

'It was nothing much,' she protested, embarrassed.

'Nonsense! Dominic told me you worked very hard, and your help was invaluable.'

'He said that?' Alexandra was amazed.

'Of course, and no doubt he would have told you so to your face, if you hadn't taken off in such a hurry! Never mind. Run along now, and enjoy yourself.'

It made Alexandra feel twelve years old again, to be scolded affectionately by Tante Corinne. Françoise steered her into the dining-room, stopping now and then to introduce her to people, all of whom, as she had said, seemed to have some important function or title, all of whom looked rich and sophisticated but chatted unpretentiously to Alexandra, without snobbery.

'Those who really have wealth or power, and are used to having it, don't need to show off,' Françoise replied sagely, when she remarked on this. 'There's one of the exceptions—Albert Paulin. Just because he owns half the wine merchants in the area, it's no excuse for behaving as if he were royalty! However, I suppose I must say a few words to the old fool.'

Alexandra saw that Monsieur Paulin inevitably had Nathalie with him, wearing a filmy white gown with *diamanté* straps showing off her perfect *décolletage*, a circlet of what had to be real diamonds around her slender neck. She was spared from having to talk to them by Michel, who swanned across the room and curled an arm round her waist.

'Cousin Alexandra! How stunning you are,' he said,

nuzzling her neck. 'Why you are not some man's wife, and the mother of six children, I can't understand.'

'Maybe because no one has asked me,' she said sweetly, fending him off.

'*Quelle dommage!* Maybe I shall propose to you myself before the evening is out!' He grinned, seizing two more glasses of champagne as a maid passed with a tray.

'Maybe you had better drink more Perrier, *mon brave*! I may accept, and then where would you be?' She grinned back. He laughed, accepting this badinage in good part, but she could tell he had already had just a little too much to drink.

Where was Dominic? Obviously he had to be here, and the more time that went by before she took the hurdle of meeting him, the harder it would be. Outside, the sky had darkened and a full, brilliant moon was climbing above the hills, a faint breeze stirring the vines. Alexandra escaped from Michel while he was busy flirting with a girl in a tea-coloured satin dress, and slipped out on to the terrace.

Everyone was indoors now, enjoying the buffet, laughing and talking, but she was not hungry, nor was there any real laughter in her heart. She wished that she could leave, now she had paid her respects to Tante Corinne, but even that was not possible. She had come with Françoise, and could not leave until she was ready to go.

'Lexi?'

She turned swiftly to find Danielle standing behind her. 'Dani!' How could she have thought of leaving, without seeing her friend? Danielle's warm cheek brushed hers, and the dark eyes, so much like her brother's, regarded her intently.

'Lexi. . .you look so sad. What's wrong?'

'Nothing.' She forced a smile to her face. 'All this is a bit much for me. So many people, all dressed to kill, so much champagne! I'm just a poor student from Oxford, remember!'

'Just a graduate with a long string of letters after her name,' Danielle said ruefully. 'You put me to shame! What have I ever done?'

'You produced that adorable little girl, didn't you? And Dominic told me you're about to increase the number. That's a real achievement—a family,' Alexandra said, trying to keep the note of wistfulness out of her voice. 'And speaking of Dominic——' she steadied herself deliberately '—where is he? I haven't seen him yet, tonight.'

'I saw him five minutes ago, going into the library with Albert Paulin,' Danielle said. 'Talking business, I suppose. He never lets up. Come on, let's eat. Having just got past the stage where I throw up all the time, I now have this burning need to consume everything that stands still!'

Alexandra accompanied her half-heartedly. Talking business? The kind of business that involved access to a chain of marketing outlets in return for a marriage contract? The kind of business that would make Nathalie Paulin Comtesse d'Albigny? Damn it, the girl was already wearing white—as if she was rehearsing the part.

She picked at a canapé, wondering why best Beluga caviare tasted indistinguishable from supermarket cods' roe. She had known that Dominic intended marrying

Nathalie. He had told her so himself, and on the surface it seemed an ideal match.

But she would bore him silly, Françoise had said. Maybe she would, but he would be meticulously faithful to her, determined not to repeat his parents' mistake, unaware that in a sense he was doing just that, in marrying someone he did not love.

Alexandra stared across the dining-room, through the wide open doors into the hall, to the door of the library beyond. She wanted to rush in and shout, 'Don't do it! You can't! Can't you see that I love you?'

But she had nothing to give, other than her love, for which he had no use. Out of the past, she heard her mother's voice saying sharply, 'We're poor relations. . .not really good enough.'

Her head went up, and she heard her own voice argue softly, but aloud, 'No. I don't believe that.'

'*Comment?*' Danielle said, puzzled, but Alexandra only smiled and said, 'Nothing. I was just thinking.'

And suddenly it was all crystal-clear to her. Glancing across the room, she saw that Françoise, too, had her gaze covertly trained on the library door, and that she was biting her lip with anxiety. She knew, and she was afraid that her son was going to make an awful mistake. Alexandra thought of Danielle and the new baby, of Michel who needed stability and serenity to help him through his wild patch, of Tante Corinne, so much better and happier tonight.

They were *not* too good for her. That was just the bitter nonsense of a disappointed woman talking. They were her dear family, whom she'd found again after much trauma; she loved them all, and couldn't bear the thought of yet another unhappy marriage plunging them back into misery and insecurity. . .another generation of children growing up under its shadow.

So she could not have Dominic. So he did not want her. Very well. But one day, perhaps, there would be a woman for him, the right woman, and their love would make Château Albigny a wonderful place for him and for all his family. If she could only avert the disaster she feared was taking place right now, behind that closed door. If she could only throw a spanner into the works for long enough to gain them a breathing space.

She looked at Françoise, met her eye, and slowly winked, as if to say—leave it to me. And then, without a word, slipped out of the room. The audacity of her impulse left her cold with horror, but she paused outside the library only long enough to unfasten the top three buttons of her bodice, and dishevel the French plait which had taken Françoise half the afternoon to do.

After this he's surely going to hate me, if he doesn't already, she thought dully. But one day, maybe, far ahead into the future—a day neither of us can yet see—he might look back and thank me. Pretty poor consolation that was to her, tonight.

Alexandra raised her hand and pushed open the library door. Over the top, she thought with wry desperation.

CHAPTER TEN

ALBERT PAULIN and Dominic were standing over by the fireplace, which tonight was filled by a huge vase of yellow, white and apricot roses. They were deeply engrossed in urgent, low-voiced conversation, and were not aware of Alexandra's entrance until she closed the door behind her.

She still had her glass of champagne in one hand, and she contrived to slop some carelessly on the floor as she sashayed across the room, swivelling her hips suggestively.

'So this is where you've been hiding yourself all evening!' She giggled accusingly, gazing up at Dominic with wide-open, adoring eyes. 'I've been here for simply ages, and haven't seen you for a minute, you naughty boy! You wouldn't be trying to avoid me, would you?'

Dominic was looking at her in mild puzzlement, his eyebrows raised. His voice was tolerant but firm as he said, 'I'm busy right now, Alexandra, as you can see. Monsieur Paulin and I were in the middle of a discussion. Why don't you go back to the party, and I'll see you in a while?'

Alexandra stretched one arm behind her head, rumpling her hair even further, the backward arch of her body thrusting her breasts forward provocatively. She gave what she hoped was a brilliantly sexy smile.

'Oh, hi there, Monsieur Paulin! You look so distinguished tonight,' she cooed. 'I think all the younger men had better watch out for some fierce competition!'

Giggling again, she took a slurp of her drink, and the fates must have been guiding her performance—either that or she had drunk it too quickly, for she actually hiccupped, a feat she could not have simulated.

Albert Paulin's face was red, he looked flustered and ill at ease.

'One can only assume that my cousin has been overindulging in the champagne,' Dominic apologised smoothly. 'Off you go, Alexandra, before you make yourself look a complete idiot.'

He put both hands on her shoulders in an attempt to turn her round, but she slid her arms round his neck, one hand still clutching the glass, and gazed into the stony face, seeing the beginnings of annoyance competing with amusement in the dark eyes.

'Oh, Dominic, *chéri!*' she wailed plaintively. 'It's a *party*, you can't shut yourself away in here talking silly old business all night! And after I've come all this way just to be with you! Give me a kiss—I won't go away until you do!'

'I suggest you have some black coffee and go lie down somewhere,' he advised coolly, and, although he appeared to go along with the notion that she was drunk, from the half-scornful expression on his face she had an awful suspicion he did not really believe it.

'Yes, yes!' she said eagerly, throwing caution to the wind. 'I'll go and lie down, but only if you'll come with me—please!' Her arms twined around his neck, and she muttered stupidly, 'Like we did at Roussillon Village, remember? You didn't send me away then, did you?' Allowing her voice to rise hysterically, she cried, 'I know why you're being so mean! There's someone else, isn't there? I know there is! Don't lie to me!'

He took hold of her wrists, disengaging her grasp. 'That's quite enough. Stop this nonsense immediately,' he ordered, and there was real anger in his eyes now. 'You're making an exhibition of yourself.'

Alexandra did not mean to drop the glass. His grip was painfully hard, and somehow it slipped from her fingers and smashed into glittering crystal fragments on the parquet floor. She knew it was expensive, and hoped it was not part of a set and irreplaceable, but, since it had happened, she wasn't above using it to add drama to her act.

'Oh, no! Now look what you've made me do!' she cried, blinking tears to her eyes. 'It's all your fault! You beast, I hate you! After what you did to me, you've got another woman, I know it! I hate you!'

Turning, she fled sobbing from the room, slamming the door resoundingly behind her. Briefly she paused in the hall, and a number of the well-heeled, well-dressed guests turned to look curiously at the distraught, wild-eyed girl.

Alexandra straightened up, dropped the act, and gave herself a little satisfied shake. Well, that should interrupt the proceedings in there, if nothing else, she thought. Perhaps Albert Paulin would think twice about marrying his daughter to a man who appeared to be embroiled in a passionate affair with someone else, even if it would make Nathalie a Comtesse! Maybe I didn't go far enough, she thought grimly—I should have hinted that Dominic was the father of my unborn child! All she had won was the briefest of respites. Would it be enough?

And then she thought about what she *had* actually done, and shuddered as she glanced over her shoulder at the library door. It remained closed. Dominic would have to mollify Monsieur Paulin, and apologise for the embarrassing spectacle his cousin had presented; but his wrath, she knew, would descend squarely on her, and very soon.

She hesitated no longer. Without consciously thinking about her actions, she hurried down the hall and out through the front door which stood open to the warm night. Once outside, she broke instinctively into a run, speeding along the path through the gardens, not stopping until she reached the temporary sanctuary of the stables. Breathless, shedding her shoes at its foot, she scrambled up the ladder into the hayloft above, and cast herself down on the prickly, sweet-scented bales of hay. And now her tears were not feigned, but in earnest.

She knew she could not hope to evade Dominic for very long. He would find her, he would be very, *very* angry, and, one way or another, he would make her pay for what she had done. She did not care about that. She did not care if he beat her black and blue before throwing her out into the night.

Only now, she wondered despairingly what she had thought to achieve with her silly little scene. Maybe things would be a little fraught, and there would be no engagement announced tonight. But, if Dominic had set his mind on marrying Nathalie, if it suited his purpose, he was not a man to be deflected easily.

And maybe Paulin was not over-concerned about his

daughter's personal happiness. It was possible he did not care how many other women her future husband kept, so long as she was suitably titled and connected.

Why did you do it? she asked herself. What difference did you think it would make? There was nothing she could do but go away, this time forever, leaving Dominic to whatever fate he had chosen. She could help neither him nor herself. Burying her face in the hay, she sobbed helplessly, heartbrokenly, until she had no tears left. It had all come to an end here, in the stables, where it had begun so many years ago.

She had cried herself out and was still lying there, inert and emotionally drained, when she heard his footstep.

'Alexandra,' he called. 'It's no use hiding—I know you're here.'

She sniffed miserably and forced herself to sit up, dragging her sleeve across her eyes and blotching her ruined make-up even more.

'Up there, are you?' he said, and she heard him climbing the ladder, saw his head and shoulders appear, and then he pulled himself up, dropping easily on to one of the bales at her side. She had expected him to be in a towering rage, almost fit to kill her, but he was strangely calm, and seemed more curious than angry.

'*Alors*, come along,' he said levelly. 'I think at the very least I deserve an explanation of that bravura act you put on just now, in the library.'

'Act?' she prevaricated, raising red-rimmed eyes cautiously, and peering through the gloom, trying but failing to read his expression.

'Well, of course, you don't seriously expect me to believe that you were drunk, do you?' he said, still in that reasonable voice she found oddly alarming. 'Although I think you had Albert Paulin fooled. He thinks you're a lush. I know you aren't. So what *was* it all about?'

She forced a nonchalant shrug. 'I. . . I wanted to interrupt your discussion.' She might as well come right out with at least a version of the truth, she reasoned, without betraying the extent to which her own emotions were involved. 'I thought you were about to. . .to make an awful mistake.'

He raised a sardonic eyebrow. 'By negotiating a deal on outlets? Since when have you become an expert on marketing, along with your many other talents?'

She winced. 'You know what I mean. By marrying Nathalie. You've gone out of your way to. . .to avoid repeating your parents' mistake, refusing to get seriously involved with any woman, but can't you see, you'd be doing *exactly* what your father did. Marrying a woman you don't love. Storing up future unhappiness for yourself. . .and for all the family. I. . . I wanted to prevent you from taking the first step in that direction, tonight. I see now that it was a stupid and futile thing for me to do,' she finished lamely.

He sat for a full minute in silence, looking at her, his eyes searching and measuring as if he was trying to seek out and pin down the essence of truth in what she said.

Finally, he said, 'I don't know what gives you the arrogance, the audacity, to think you're entitled to meddle in my affairs. If you ever had that right, you forfeited it the day you ran out on me at Roussillon Village. A one-night stand doesn't qualify you to interfere with my life.'

She gave an incredulous gasp. 'Ran out on you?' she repeated accusingly. 'I don't know how you can say that! It was you who sent me away, after you'd had all you wanted from me! You left a delightfully clear message that I wasn't required any more, and I felt as soiled and unwanted as. . .as a worn, cast-off shoe! It's you who are the one-night stand expert!'

'The message I left was that there was no longer any need for you to knock yourself out working, not that you should leave,' he said exasperatedly. 'You had put so much into it, all week, I reckoned you must be exhausted. And——' the suggestion of a smile played on his lips '—into the bargain, we'd had rather an energetic night.'

She knew her skin was reddening, burning with the all too vivid memories of making love with him. It was unfair of him to allude to it.

'Who are you kidding? You wanted me to be gone by the time you got back!' she cried, low-voiced. 'I expect you thought I was going to make a fuss over what had happened. Well, I wasn't. And I'm not now. It was just. . .just one of those things. You were tense and wound up over Tante Corinne's illness, so was I, and. . .that's all there was to it.'

Suddenly and unexpectedly he gripped both her wrists, even harder than he had done back in the library, so that she flinched from the pain, but he did not release her.

'I've had enough of this fencing and fooling around,' he said fiercely. 'Let's have some truth between us, if that's all we can hope to have! "One of those things", was it? I'm no novice, I've made love to. . .well, a number of women. Nor are you. But tell me——' If it was humanly possible, his grip tightened, but she no longer felt any pain—she was looking deep into his eyes, returning that intently searching stare. '*Tell me,*' he repeated insistently, 'have you ever before been close to the heights we reached that night? Did Tristan ever make you feel you were about to die in his arms? Is this a commonplace experience for you? Because it certainly isn't for me!'

The truth between us? Slowly, honestly, she shook her head, and her voice broke a little as she confessed, 'No. Never in my life. . .never, Dominic. I didn't even know there was such feeling.'

He released her wrists and gave a low groan as his hands framed her face, drawing her mouth towards his, and she let him take her lips, readily, all the longing and loneliness of the endless winter melting away at the touch of him. She felt his fingers deftly working their way down the buttons of her bodice, and twin rivers of pleasure and need flowed through her. She wanted him to make love to her—wanted it desperately—but at the same time knew she could not endure to be transported once again to that magical kingdom, and then cast out. His passion matched hers, but it wasn't enough if she could not have his love.

'No!' she gasped. 'Please, Dominic, no, not again! No more! I can't bear it!'

His hands arrested themselves on her shoulders as he heard the despair in her voice, and saw in a sudden shaft of moonlight from the high loft windows that her face was tear-streaked. Gently, he touched her cheek and found it damp. Folding her tenderly in his arms, he rocked her to and fro, stroking her hair.

'Don't cry, Lexi,' he said softly. 'Right now, I want

more than anything to be your lover again, but you needn't fear. I'll not be second best, if you're still pining for him. I would rather be simply your cousin, your friend—as I have always been.'

Still in his arms, she wriggled a little so that she could look up into his face, and she was surprised by the sadness and resignation transforming the usually arrogant features. A thought hovered, only inches away from her grasp, but it was too grandiose, too earth-shattering, too utterly revolutionary for her to give it words.

The truth between us?

'For *him*?' she repeated. 'You mean Tristan?' She shook her head. 'I was over that long ago—probably before I left here in October, although perhaps I didn't know it at the time. And, if it gives you any satisfaction, you were right. He didn't love me. He used me, and I wasn't the first.'

'It gives me no satisfaction,' he told her. 'But I'm glad you exorcised the ghost. So why the tears? You're a free woman.'

'The tears are for *you*, cousin Dominic,' she told him bitterly. 'Because you keep on rejecting me when I need you. . .and you're all set to do it over again!'

'*Mais non!*' he said with deep indignation. 'You are the most beautiful, the most fascinating, the most pigheaded and infuriating woman I have ever known! *Je t'aime*—lord help me, I love you! Wasn't that what I was trying to make you understand?'

Alexandra sat very still, but inside her something joyful and incredulous leapt vibrantly to life. Dominic loved her? She did not dare trust the swelling, rapturous feelings of hope and happiness enveloping her. It must be a trick, an illusion. She would pinch herself soon and wake up.

'But you don't believe in love,' she said, her cautious, finely tuned mind refusing to accept this tremendous gift at its face-value.

'That, *ma chérie*, is like continuing to believe the earth is flat when you've seen the satellite pictures of it revolving in space,' he told her ruefully. 'I didn't want to believe it. I did my damndest to resist it, ever since you came back here invading my well-organised existence. But it happened.'

He sighed. 'I found myself being insanely jealous of a dead man! Hating him for how he had almost wrecked your sanity, yet resenting the loyalty you still felt you owed him. There was no way I could fight this ghost. Then, at Roussillon Village, I thought at last you were mine. All I did was to take an hour to visit *Grand-mère*, thinking you would not even wake before I returned, but when I got back...*voila*! My elusive bird had flown. I spent most of the winter trying to talk myself out of love, and when you came back, although I couldn't wait to see you again, the only weapon I had was to try and hate you for leaving me before.'

'Dominic, I was so confused, last autumn—you upset every preconception about love and life that I ever had,' she said urgently. 'I told myself I couldn't possibly be in love with you. As soon as I got back to England, everything started to fall into place in my mind, and I knew for certain that I was—that this was the real thing, not the imitation. But you had told me you intended to marry Nathalie——'

She gasped, put her hands out to fend him off, just as he was about to draw her closer. 'Oh, Dominic—

that business in the library, with Monsieur Paulin—did I really mess it up for you?'

He grinned. 'Now, Lexi, do be logical. Wasn't that exactly what you intended to do?'

'Yes, but your deal. . .the marketing outlets. . .'

'Hang the outlets,' he said succinctly. 'Château Albigny will survive without them. For your information, yes, I'd toyed with the idea of marrying Nathalie, but when it came right down to it, I couldn't face the thought of a lifetime with her. . .particularly having got to know *you* once more. It would be like marrying a Barbie Doll! I think I only told you that as a. . .a defence against falling in love with you, and, as such, it failed miserably.'

'But in the library——' she persisted.

'Albert Paulin asked to see me privately,' he told her. 'He made me an offer—one which did include his daughter. But I turned it down, *chérie*. Before you came into the library. There was no need for that delightful burlesque of yours. . .fascinating as it was!'

She gave a shriek of outrage, and then collapsed into helpless laughter. 'I did all that for nothing? Well, of all the——' she began.

He drew her gently down on to the fragrant hay and began kissing her. 'Never mind about all that, now. Tell me you love me. And only me.'

'I love you. Only you. I loved you when I was fifteen. You didn't care for me very much then, as I remember,' she told him, eyes laughing.

'I—cared—very—much,' he said, punctuating each word with a kiss. 'But you were too young for what it was all leading up to. Damn it, Lexi, you were underage! I didn't dare let it start, for fear that if it did we wouldn't be able to stop. I thought we should wait. I thought that when you came back, the next summer, you would be older. . .and we'd see if we still felt the same way.'

'But I never did come back,' she said soberly. 'All those years I thought you hadn't wanted me, that I wasn't pretty enough. You broke my heart, cousin Dominic—I'll see you pay for that!'

'In any coin you like,' he agreed. 'I have the perfect repayment scheme. Can I start the instalments right away?'

She wound her arms round him, holding him very close. 'Oh, Dominic, so many years, so much misunderstanding.' She sighed. 'I go cold all over, just thinking how nearly we didn't make it.'

'But we did,' he said, his lips against her throat. 'Never leave me, Alexandra. With you I can learn to trust, to know that love can bring happiness as well as pain. From now on, I, and Château Albigny, belong to you. This is your rightful place.'

Some time later, Dominic and Alexandra walked quietly back through the gardens, hand in hand, she still barefoot and carrying the shoes she had shed at the foot of the ladder. Avoiding the crowd, they slipped in silently through a door at the back of the house. He paused to kiss her, lingeringly, and she clung to him, both of them unwilling to let go of the happiness they had so recently tasted.

At last he sighed and said, 'Go up to your old bedroom and put some more warpaint on your face. I'll ask my mother to come up and tidy your hair, if she can control her delight at the prospect of having you for a daughter-in-law! Between the two of you, I can see I shall be well henpecked.'

'You? Never.' She brushed his jacket lightly with one hand. 'But you could do with a bit of a tidy-up yourself, I must say. Why all the fuss?'

He bent and kissed the tip of her nose. 'Because, my love, we have an announcement to make. And members of the Press are here.' He grinned, the wicked piratical grin she loved. 'As far as I am concerned, you look divine, just as you are. But we don't want the future Comtesse d'Albigny appearing in tomorrow's papers with straw in her hair, do we? Hurry up, now. I'm impatient. If you're absent from me for longer than five minutes, I shall want to know why.'

Alexandra smiled back. 'Five minutes without you will be as much as I can take,' she promised. '*Au revoir*, Monsieur le Comte—my love.'

And, noiselessly, shoes in her hand, straw in her hair, she sped upstairs.

A PASSIONATE LOVE

**THURSDAY AND THE LADY
– Patricia Matthews** £3.50

A story of a proud and passionate love as tempestuous as the age that created it.

A woman journalist working on the first magazine published for women is torn between two men – one who stirs her passions and another who shares her beliefs.

September 1990

W☉RLDWIDE

Available from Boots, Martins, John Menzies, W.H. Smith, Woolworths and other paperback stockists.

Also available from Reader Service, P.O. Box 236, Thornton Road, Croydon, Surrey CR9 3RU

2 COMPELLING READS FOR AUGUST 1990

HONOUR BOUND – Shirley Larson £2.99

The last time Shelly Armstrong had seen Justin Corbett, she'd been a tongue tied teenager overwhelmed by his good looks and opulent lifestyle. Now she was an accomplished pilot with her own flying school, and equal to Justin in all respects but one – she was still a novice at loving.

SUMMER LIGHTNING – Sandra James £2.99

The elemental passions of *Spring Thunder* come alive again in the sequel . . .
Maggie Howard is staunchly against the resumption of logging in her small Oregon town – McBride Lumber had played too often with the lives of families there. So when Jared McBride returned determined to reopen the operation, Maggie was equally determined to block his every move – whatever the cost.

WORLDWIDE

Available from Boots, Martins, John Menzies, W.H. Smith, Woolworths and other paperback stockists.

Zodiac Wordsearch Competition

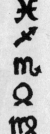

How would you like a years supply of Mills & Boon Romances ABSOLUTELY FREE?

Well, you can win them! All you have to do is complete the word puzzle below and send it into us by Dec 31st 1990. The first five correct entries picked out of the bag after this date will each win a years supply of Mills & Boon Romances (Six books every month - worth over £100!) What could be easier?

S	E	C	S	I	P	R	I	A	M	F
I	U	L	C	A	N	C	E	R	L	I
S	A	I	N	I	M	E	G	N	S	R
C	A	P	R	I	C	O	R	N	U	E
S	E	I	R	A	N	G	I	S	I	O
Z	O	D	W	A	T	E	R	B	R	I
O	G	A	H	M	A	T	O	O	A	P
D	R	R	T	O	U	N	I	R	U	R
I	I	B	R	O	R	O	M	G	Q	O
A	V	I	A	N	U	A	N	C	A	C
C	E	L	E	O	S	T	A	R	S	S

- Pisces
- Cancer
- Scorpio
- Aquarius
- Capricorn
- Aries
- Gemini
- Taurus
- Libra
- Sagittarius
- Leo
- Virgo
- Fire
- Water
- Zodiac
- Earth
- Star
- Sign
- Moon
- Air

Please turn over for entry details

☆ How to enter ☆

All the words listed overleaf, below the word puzzle, are hidden in the grid. You can can find them by reading the letters forwards, backwards, up and down, or diagonally. When you find a word, circle it, or put a line through it. After you have found all the words, the left-over letters will spell a secret message that you can read from left to right, from the top of the puzzle through to the bottom.

Don't forget to fill in your name and address in the space provided and pop this page in an envelope (you don't need a stamp) and post it today. Competition closes Dec 31st 1990.

Only one entry per household (more than one will render the entry invalid).

Mills & Boon Competition
Freepost
P.O. Box 236
Croydon
Surrey CR9 9EL

Hidden message _____

_____

Are you a Reader Service subscriber.   Yes ❑   No ❑

Name _____

Address _____

_____

_____

_____ **Postcode** _____

You may be mailed with other offers as a result of entering this competition.
If you would prefer not to be mailed please tick the box. No ❑

COMP9